To Durchhalten

(Durk-hal-tən)

By

Carlene Meredith Cogliati

Elizabeth Hawk Publishing
Lake Charles, LA
2018

C. M. Cogliati

Thank you to my editing team:
Erika Meidl, Rachael Mohatt & Michele Macy
And especially Donna H. Regehr

Cover by Paigeosity & C.M. Cogliati

Published by Elizabeth Hawk Publishing
www.elizabethhawkpublishing.com
Lake Charles, LA
2018

ISBN – 13:978-1986076258
ISBN-10:1986076253

For Tucker and Leslie.
Your Mom loved this story, for itself and for those it can touch.
And Cass; I will love you always.

Dear Readers,
Please note that the formatting peculiarities are intentional. I wrote this as closely as I could to the voice of a pre-teen girl & the way she would write a journal.

C. M. Cogliati

6th Grade

Thursday, Sept. 2nd

YEA ! I'm finally Here! My name is Amy Dixon and I'm in the 6th grade now. That means I've moved to the next classroom, in with the 7th and 8th graders. Yes! Ta Da Da DAT Da DA! I like to figure out how to spell made up words. I like words and spelling, period. I guess Mr. Moore had heard that because when we got this assignment (to keep a journal all year) he said we needed to write something every day, then looking straight at me he added, "You can write as much as you like, but I will only be doing corrections on one page."

I can't help it that I like to write. There's just so much to say. Even when things seem dull, I get started and suddenly I'm out of time and still have more to say. Jesse says I blither - [(**bli**·thər) - To speak or utter foolish babble, to jabber.]

The first time he said it I thought it sounded like blizzard, and pictured a storm of white words swirling around me. Jesse said I wasn't far off.

He's not bad for a brother though. He's an 8th grader so this is his last year here, BOO HISS. He and Alan and Gibb, Kayleen and C.C. will all be going to town to high school next year; that's an hour away.

We hate it when anyone leaves. Boulder Point is such a small school; we're kind of like a big family. Some people really are related (like the Abercrombies and Abernathys) but it seems like we all are. I keep seeing back-to-school commercials where the kids hate school starting again, but I don't. Everyone is spread out so much through the mountain ridges that we aren't able to get together much during the summer, so by September we're really jazzed to come back and see everybody.

Yesterday was the first day of school. We didn't do much, mostly played and got our rooms organized. Mr. Moore passed out our books. I got Jesse's old math book. I love it when I get a book he had. I didn't get any last year. I got another surprise too.

Glancing at the list of previous names inside the cover, I saw Andrea Corbit, Arthur's big sister. Arthur is partly responsible for my interest in spelling AND the Spelling Bee. Goodness, that is such a hugely important part of my life! Who would have thought it when I first started school here?

Anyway, his sister had this book when she was in 6th grade – that would have been her last year here, back when I hated Arthur instead of Jonathan. I was in 4th grade with Mrs. Olsen. She has the 3rd through 5th graders.

The door between our rooms is open right now. I see can Kitty and Shereese, D.D. and Anna all whispering together. Wonder what they're saying. Hmm, Shereese just giggled, I can tell even though I can't hear it. She has a great giggle. I snort. At least Jesse says I do. Heather says I have a <u>great</u> laugh. Wish I was laughing with them now.

Oh well, I'm over here, in the cool room. The one with all the microscopes and animals. Everyone gets to visit the animals sometimes but only the biggest kids get to take care of them now. The other two rooms used to have animals too, but Mr. Goodwin got tired of taking care of them when the kids didn't (he takes care of everything else around here as it is) and tired of hunting for Miles when his cage got left open.

"Miles can slither straight up the side of his cage," Mr. Goodwin said over and over. "You HAVE to keep the lid closed."

Ring is too small to get out, but both cages got moved after a fat Miles was found in the gerbil cage with no gerbils left.

The fish used to be in Mrs. Mitchell's room. When I was in Kindergarten, Kevin Abercrombie would always dump a whole box of fish food into the tank. Mrs. Mitchell tried and tried to stop him. "But they're so hungry," Kevin would whine. "Their poor little sides are all flat." Mrs. Mitchell would explain and explain that was the way they were supposed to be and even showed him pictures. Kevin was not convinced. "They have such big, sad eyes and they always swim over to watch me eat my snack."

"So don't eat by them," she frowned. But the morning after Mr. Goodwin found half a peanut-butter sandwich in the tank, the fish moved. Kevin is in 7th grade now and finally gets to take care of the fish. No more gummy guppies.

Gotta go. Time for math, then spelling. Yea spelling!

P.S.   Jonathan is <u>such</u> a snot! Jerk! CREEP! He stole my math book! He won't admit it but I know it was him.

Friday, Sept. 3rd

I can't believe it's Friday already. Mr. Moore said to keep a piece of paper handy this weekend to write descriptive words on - not sentences, just words or phrases.

[(frāz) n. A group of two or more associated words, not containing a subject or a predicate.]

Then on Tuesday, we will each write a poem about Labor Day.

He said this journal has several purposes. First, it's good exercise and discipline for the mind to write. Kind of like doing daily laps for the body. Second, when we are old like him (he said that), it will be lots of fun to read and remember this time.

Third, and most important, it will be a good place
to sort out our thoughts and feelings. We can't
write honestly if we aren't honest with ourselves.
"To thine own self be true," he said. Mr. Moore is
very smart. Jesse told me he was a good teacher.
And no, I didn't write that because you will read it
sometime, Mr. Moore. It just came to mind, so I
wrote it.

But, back to work. "Try to describe something
each day; a thought, or emotion; an event or
observation."

I'm observing. I'm observing Heather. Her
long shiny hair swings down on each side of her
face. (It's not as long as mine, but she hopes it
will catch up.) Chin on hand, she is gazing out the
large windows at the schoolyard. A smile tugs at
her mouth, a bigger smile. She slaps both hands
over her mouth. Catching my eye, she motions
out the window.

Ooh – Big Mama is grazing out there with
her fawns. She is munching away at the grass
on the playground while this year's set of twins
frolic around. Two rows of fuzzy white spots

line their little sides. Large dark eyes sparkle alertly. At the lightest sound they prance sideways on spindly legs. Big Mama has worked her way to the far apple tree. As she eats from an apple hanging there, another falls. The babies flee. Big Mama doesn't move. The twins come back, sniffing, jumping back. I don't believe they are really afraid, more like kids enjoying scaring themselves with ghost stories. Oops – they're gone. Mr. Goodwin came out of his house on the other side of the parking lot and they took off.

P.S. I snuck a peek in Jonathan's desk at lunch but no book. I know he's hidden it somewhere.

Tuesday, Sept. 7th

Simmering sun, beating down

Turning skin all pink and brown.

Rounded stones beneath my feet

Cold and icy in the deep.

Watch the river spirits race,

Warm my back and cool my face.

Moms and Dads and kids galore,

Cousins rolling on the floor.

Bar-B-Que and have a feast,

Apple pie and roasted beast.

Spread the bedrolls on the lawn,

Now the sun is dark and gone.

Watch the stars come out and play,

End of summer, Labor Day.

Wednesday, Sept. 8th

Jesse's not wearing his hoodie. That shows you how hot it is. Hot, fot, sot, soppy, lots of hotty hot. Makes me want to go back to the river.

Even without closing my eyes I can see the water rippling over the shallows, flashing in the sun. We - Jesse, our cousins and I, and of course Uncle Jon, (he likes doing kid things more than adult things) lay there, letting the river splash over our shoulders and under us, tumbling and washing us downstream to the swimming hole, laughing the whole way. Then walking back upstream, we did it again and again.

I'm so hot. The ceiling fan is whooshing away over us. I think I would die if it went off. My sweaty hand is sticking to the paper and my pencil doesn't write very well on the damp paper. I've had to wipe off my hand and pencil three times already. Maybe I shouldn't have run races at lunch. That book-stealing rat always wins anyway.

Thursday, Sept. 9th

Mom's here today. **YEA!** She usually comes and helps Tuesdays and Thursdays. Mostly she reads with the little kids but today everyone started our herptile research.

[Herptile (Hurp·tīl) *n*. All members of the reptile and amphibian families.]

All three class groups wanted to visit Ring and Miles. Ring is only 4 inches long; about the size of an earthworm, only cuter. A lot. And cleaner. He feels like a little silk rope slipping through my fingers. Seeing only his shiny black back as he moves around in his cage, new kids are surprised at his bright orange belly, which matches the thin ring around his neck. Mom found him a couple of years ago and brought him in so everyone could play with him and learn not to be afraid of snakes. That's my Mom, always thinking of others.

Miles is a bit bigger. Just a bit. Like 5 Feet! He's a Boa Constrictor and used to belong to Mr. Goodwin's sons but after they grew up and got married, neither of their wives wanted him around, so Miles lives here now.

First thing this morning everyone trooped into our room and sat cross-legged in a circle on the rug. Mom likes to take them out early while it's cool and our cold-blooded friends are still stiff and slow. After lunch when it's hot, they get really frisky and move so fast they can even make the big kids jump.

The older students held Ring first so the little kids could see how much they liked it and weren't afraid.

Of course Shane Olsen wasn't afraid. He's visited his mom's class a lot and he <u>loves</u> Ring. Shereese is such a clown. She used to tease her little brother about Ring. "Mmmm, doesn't he look delicious? I could just eat him up." She'd open her mouth and dangled Ring over her. "Ahhh." Poor Shane would scream and jump, flailing his little arms against her. Then she got caught. Mrs. Olsen seemed a foot taller, glowering down at her daughter with steam coming out of her ears. I'm sure glad it wasn't me.

Today, after everyone held Ring, it was Miles' turn. Mom sat in the middle of our circle and gently held his head as he curled around her arm. Everyone took turns going up and petting him. New kids expect snakes to be slimy and gross, but

they're not. Sleek, I would say, smooth and silky.
Miles is big enough that each of his scales shows,
overlapping like perfect shingles, undulating with
his every move.   [Undulate (**UN**·dy·**lāt**) *v.* to move
like a wave or in waves.]

    After the snakes went back in their homes our
class wrote about what we'd observed. That's when
I looked up undulate. In third grade I would get
really frustrated about not knowing the right
words to express myself. So Mrs. Olsen showed
me the thesaurus and I learned it wasn't a dinosaur
but a wonderful book of words. Then she had me
look up new words in the dictionary to make sure I
really understood them, then I wrote them down
so I'd remember. I still do that. She's a smart
teacher. All of our teachers are, Ms. Pascalla too.
She's a lot more than a secretary and bus driver.
I've never asked her a question she couldn't answer.

    Mom stays for lunch the days she's here. She's
so great, everyone thinks so. When she came out
to the picnic tables, almost everyone tried to make
a space for her next to them. "Here Mrs. Dixon,
there's a place here."

    "Thanks," she told them all with a smile, "but I
think I'll eat here today." And she put her lunch by
Heather and me.

E.S. jumped up. "Mrs. Dixon, Mrs. Dixon, I gotta show you," and he ran off. I guess the youngest class drew pictures this morning. He came back with his. Ring was a wiggly black line with a fat red crayon stripe across his neck. Miles was a pile of squiggly lines under the smiley face he'd drawn for my mom. I know it was her because of the long hair he'd drawn. She has really gorgeous long hair, even longer than mine. I love it. Mom smiled enthusiastically. "That's wonderful, E.S. That looks just like Miles, and no one could mistake Ring either, good job." He just beamed.

Mon. Sept. 13th

Friday was swim day (Yes, Yes, YES!) so we'd left our journals for Mr. Moore to check over.

Every other Friday we ride the bus the hour long trip to town and have an outing. It isn't always the same place, sometimes a performance or something, but most often it's the library. I love libraries and the special smell of thousands of books as they sit expectantly on the shelves, waiting for someone to choose <u>them</u> to read. I picture them jumping up and down, like puppies in a pet store, "Me, me, pick me!"

We all spread out, each of us searching for information on the herptile we'd chosen for a special report. I am doing zee crocodile.

[crocodile (**KROK**·ə·dīl) *n.* A large, lizard like, amphibious reptile.]

There is a picnic and play area next to the library. A great place for lunch. Usually anyway. But Jonathan snagged my cupcake just as I was reaching for it and took off. I sprang after him so fast the lace trim on my shirt caught on the corner of the table. I could feel it rip as I tore after that slimy thief. He climbed up the slippery-slide the wrong way and I whacked my right shin chasing him. He was heading for the tubes and I know he would have gotten away if Heather hadn't helped me. She snatched it out of his hand while he was distracted, watching me trying to climb up the slide.

It was a little smooshed but I ate it slowly, where Jonathan could see me, relishing each bite with loud, exaggerated mmmms and smackings. I

was sooo mad about my shirt though, not to
mention my throbbing leg.

After lunch had time to digest, we went
swimming. Yea Swimming! Ya da da dut du DA!
Since most of us live close to the river, our
principal (Mrs. Mitchell is the principal too)
decided long ago that learning to swim was
essential for us.

[Essential (e·SEN·shul) adj. Something
fundamental and basic; cannot be done without.]

I love the water and swimming. Mom says I
swim like a fish.

Wait a minute, are fish herptiles? Maybe I
should have chosen fish to report on.

Tues. Sept. 14th

Mom's here. I saw her in the office talking to
Ms. Pascalla. I started to go in but they looked
sooo serious; I decided not to. I rarely see her
look so serious unless I've really messed up about
something.

OH! Crocodiles swim too, Mom said so at lunch. Jesse said, "Ahhh, go ahead and change to a fish Amy, and _I'll_ be the crocodile. Crocodiles EAT fish." Then he pulled the hood of his hoodie so that it hid his face and chased me around the playground, sleeves flopping over the ends of his hands, arms outstretched in front of his face, snapping at me. Alan, Gibb and some others started in too, chasing anyone who would run and scream.

I'm hot now. The cool gray of the tile floor looks inviting to lie on. The hair that fell out of my long braid is sticking to my neck and forehead. A blop of sweat just landed on my paper. Then to top it off – I found out fish are not herptiles. All that running wasted. Oh well, almost math time anyway.

I'm still using the second book Mr. Moore gave me. I refuse to write my name in it though. It's not _MY_ book. It's just a temporary loan until I figure out how to get mine back from Jon the Jerk. Maybe some unripe persimmon will have to find its way into his sandwich. Oooo OOO! I just glanced over and he gave me the most horrid grin and slowly took out the math book, watching me the whole time, wriggling his eyebrows! I could just snatch it and smack him over the head!

Wed. Sept. 15th

Time to think about Halloween, seen, sheen,
keen. Mrs. Mitchell announced it at lunch today.
I know it's early, but everyone needs to start
thinking about what they are going to do so we can
practice enough to properly amaze our audience.
We didn't talk about the program though. Heather
wanted to know what I'd be, and her cousin, Kitty,
did too. Maybe we can be the same thing.

Maybe not though. A lot of the time the
Abercrombies and Abernathys like to come as the
same thing. They're all cousins, the kids anyway.
Dave and Don Abernathy are brothers and their
sister, Heather's mom, married an Abercrombie.
The whole group calls themselves "The Aberrations
Absolute." The year before last they were all
ghosts with one black eye and a blacked out tooth.

Oops, been passing notes with Heather and now
it's time for math.

Thurs. Sept. 16th

"Yea Mom!" That's me. "Yea Mom!" That's Heather.
Jesse and I are staying over there Fri. night.

He and Kyle (Kyle graduated last year) are friends and Heather and I, well what can I say about Heather and I? She often says that I am an 'Aberration Absolute' too, since we are really sisters. She calls my parents Mom and Dad and I call hers, Mommy 'A' and Daddy 'A'. Then there's Terrible Tory, as bad as any little brother could be. Fun, run, sun, ton 'o fun and see the Bun Bun. That's Heather's bunny, and he's such a cute fuzzy bun bun too. A soft, warm, cuddly fuzz ball, scrunching down under our chins to snuggle.

I'm going to Heather's!!!

Mom said she had something to take care of in town. She's going to catch a ride with Mrs. Cardoza, Jonathan and Marie's mom. (Maybe I'll tell Mom about the math book and she can tell Mrs. Cardoza) Anyway, she'll meet up with Dad in town. Since he goes into work at the bakery so early, he gets off early. She usually does errands on swim Fridays so she can swim too. I wonder what she's doing. Jesse asked why they would be getting back so late. I kicked at him under the lunch table, showed snarly teeth and slashed my finger across my throat. What if she should decide she didn't need to be so late? Jesse made a weird scrunchy face back, but didn't kick back at me. No matter though. Her answer was, "Your dad and I thought we'd go out to dinner afterwards." YES! They should do that more anyway. Maybe I should bring my swimsuit, it's still warm enough to go to the river. What else? Blue Beary of course, but what clothes? I'll need to pack a bag tonight and bring it on the bus tomorrow.

Fri. Sept. 17th

First school spelling bee of the year. I WON! What a HUGE, TREMEDOUS SURPRIZE!!! OK, OK, forgive the sarcasm. It just gets a little boring when I win all the time.

Mom came in this morning to pass Mr. Toad around. He lives under an old sink out behind our chicken house. Lumpy, bumpy, all grayish-brown, just the color of dirt. He's so fat that even with all my fingers outstretched, he overlaps my hand.

Once again the little kids were surprised to find he wasn't slimy. Then Mom pointed out an even more surprising feature - his eyes. They are gold. Not a smooth, flat gold like a ring, but like the sample of gold flakes we have sealed inside a plexiglas cube. It is interesting to watch his slow blink unveil such glittering treasures, and to see attitudes instantly change from, "Ewww, yuck, what a gross blob," to "Oooo, wow, isn't he gorgeous."

Jesse asked Mom this morning when we would get picked up tomorrow. Why doesn't he knock it off about ending our visit before it's even started!

Kitty and Shereese want to do something for the Halloween program with Heather and I. Kayleen and C.C. think we should do something with them so we can work on it in class. It's flattering to be asked by the older girls, but they don't want Kitty and Shereese included. C.C. pointed out that we couldn't work on it in the allotted class time if it was all six of us.

I miss Kitty and Shereese. We see each other on the bus, but it's not the same as being in the same room. We can't pass notes or see the thousand silly things Shereese does every day. They'll be over here next year, but that's so far away. It's the pits.

NO! No, no, no. It's Friday! It's a gorgeous day and I am spending the night with Heather. NOTHING is going to spoil it! Not even that horrid Jonathan. I was able to totally ignore his obnoxiousness at lunch. He was running around like a maniac, throwing football passes and yelling directions to his invisible team - as no one else was playing with him. What an idiot.

Mon. Sept. 20th

Friday was sooo great, but too short. The Terrible Tory spent the night with his cousins across the road. He switched with Kitty, who came and stayed with Heather and me. YEA! We dug all through their dress-up things and Mommy 'A' let us look through her stuff too AND wear make-up. It's harder than it looks. I've gotten pretty good at putting on lipstick but I blinked at the wrong time and stuck the mascara brush in my eye. Of course, tears made it run and it all had to come off so I could start again. Kitty couldn't keep the lipstick inside the lines of her mouth. She tried wiping it off but her skin was still red so Heather went back and made her whole mouth look bigger and poochier so she had big, kissy lips.

Every time we would squeal or guffaw,
[(**guf**·fah) n. A loud burst of boisterous laughter.]
Jesse and Kyle would stick their heads in then roll
their eyes.

We decided to surprise everyone by coming
to dinner all dressed up fancy, and speaking with
English accents. However, <u>we</u> got the surprise.
I'd heard the guys giggling and snorting but that's
nothing unusual. When we opened the bedroom
door to come down though, there stood Jesse,
Kyle AND Daddy 'A', dressed up too! Ties, hats
and using sticks for canes! In a hilariously awful
English accent Daddy 'A' asked, "Would yew fwine
lydies dew us the 'onnah of joining us fo' dinnah?"
Then sticking out their arms, they escorted us to
the table.

Mommy 'A' was wearing a big frilly hat with
flowers topped by a little bird. We were most
proper and British until the bird popped off the
hat and rolled down the brim and somersaulted
into the mashed potatoes! We were all trying
desperately to maintain our decorum, reserve,
etc. when she plucked it out with her pinky aloft
saying, "Eeew, you poor silli thing, will you nevah
learn to fly?" Poor Heather lost it and snorted

milk out her nose and all was in disarray.
[(**DIS**·ə·rā) *n.* - Lack of orderly arrangement;
disorder, confusion.]

We never got anything figured out for
Halloween. I was hoping to stay longer on
Saturday and talk about it but Dad was there
right after breakfast and we had to go.

I was surprised that Mom was just getting up
when we got home. I thought they must have been
out <u>really</u> late but she said no. I sat there and told
her all about our English dinner as she finished
getting dressed. I noticed a band-aide on her
chest and I was going to ask her about it when I
finished talking about dinner, but I forgot.

Tues. Sept. 21st

This morning we looked at frogs and
salamanders. Jonathan is doing his report on
salamanders and brought in an "Ambystoma
Gracile Gracile." Good Grief! He sounded like
Arthur! It's just a common Brown Salamander!

Then he oh so proudly announced that there are at least 55 different kinds of salamanders in California alone and, "Did you know newts are actually salamanders?" He's sooo annoying! I'd better read more about crocodiles and worry less about Halloween. I will NOT be out-done by that book-thieving slimeball.

Wed. Sept. 22nd

ERRRRRrrr!

At lunch Mrs. Mitchell suggested that for the Halloween program we might want to keep to groups in our own rooms so it would be easier to rehearse. Kayleen looked so smug and self-satisfied I could have spit at her! I don't want to do ANYTHING with her! Grumble, rumble, rent and roar, gnash and gash and trash. Teeth for tearing, tongue for swearing, Rent and Dent and Smash some more!

Thurs. Sept. 23rd

WELL knock me down!!!
After lunch Jonathan challenged me to a race.
I know he's faster than me. He's always been
faster and I probably wouldn't have accepted,
except for the book. He said if I won he would
trade me math books. I <u>couldn't</u> say no. His
friend, Nathan, waited at the finish line, (Yeah,
like <u>that's</u> going to be fair) and at the other end
of the playground, Heather dropped her arm to
start us off. As expected, Jonathan leaped ahead,
but rather than continuing to pull away, he seemed
to slow down, or maybe I did speed up because I
was able to stay even with him. I glanced over and
caught him looking at me. Real fast he looked
forwards again, kind of flushed. I guess from the
effort because he surged forwards. I thought it
was all over but then I started catching up again!
And pulled passed him!!! Nathan was yelling for
Jonathan, Heather was yelling for me, then others
were shouting and suddenly I was across the line
ahead of Jonathan - I won! I couldn't believe it.
When I went back inside our classroom, the math
book was already on my desk and a warm glow crept
up from my toes to the roots of my hair.

Mom came and read with the little kids today but didn't stay for lunch. Hmmm.

Fri. Sept. 24th

Oops, I forgot to leave my journal for Mr. Moore. Oh well. Jounce, bounce, pounce. Mom came to school this morning before we left, but when I saw her in the office, Mrs. Mitchell looked upset. Not mad, but concerned and almost like she was going to cry. I hope she's OK.

Mom rode with her instead of coming on the bus with us. Guess she thought Mrs. Mitchell might need to talk. Mom was very distracted while helping me hunt new crocodile information. She looked like I probably do when I'm thinking of something else and the words on a page just melt away and I drift off somewhere else. I didn't ask her where she was. I wanted to but didn't. At breakfast this morning she asked if we would mind staying over at Abercrombie's again. Mind?! Absurdities. Two Fridays in a row! Heather is in the bus seat behind me, shooting spitballs through her lunch straw into my hair. I guess she is tired of me writing.

Sat. 25

I know it's not a school night but it is so quiet and strange feeling tonight that I feel like writing.

First things first. Last night – no, I really don't care to talk about that. It was fine and all and we got to stay at Heather's until late Sat. morning. I guess that was this morning, huh. Probably could have stayed later but Jesse felt like we should get back, so Dad came and got us. Dad, twice in a row. Usually Mom picks us up.

She was still in bed when we got home. I was worried she was sick, but she said, "No, last week I had the doctor take a little brown spot off my chest that was bothering me. It turns out that it was something that could have made me sick, so the doctor took a bigger sample, to make sure he had gotten it all. It just left me a little more tired than I expected."

She did get up but looked kind of stiff and sore. Her hair was all tangley and she said it was really uncomfortable to raise her arm to brush it. So I carefully brushed it all out, nice and silky-smooth. Then I tied it back with a big bow. After that though, she mostly sat in the big swing in the front flower garden.

Dad fixed dinner AND cleaned up. He's out watering the garden now. Jesse offered to help but Dad said, "That's OK, I could use the quiet." Mom went to bed early so I don't want to watch TV, it might wake her up. I went to Jesse's door to see if he wanted to play Scrabble. He was staring out the window with such a glazed, faraway look that I didn't figure he would hear me anyway. So here I am. Maybe I'll just read.

Mon. Sept. 27

It's really good to be back at school. Noise and energy and even an argument is nice to hear. Jesse was up fixing breakfast this morning. He did okay. The bacon was kind of crisp in the middle and fatty on the ends but the eggs were great, no soupy whites around the yolks and the edges weren't crackly crisp either.

Even though Mom got up and ate with us, she didn't walk down to the bus. Jesse was just fine in the house, then, by the time we got to the gate he was gone. His body was there and all, you know – 'the light's on but nobody's home.' Actually I'm not even sure the light was on under that hood of his.

Tues. Sept. 28th

A repeat of yesterday morning. I asked Jesse
if he was going to be a Zombie for Halloween. "No,
why?" he asked.

"Well you've certainly got the zoned out look
down pat." I thought he might get irritated, hoped
maybe, but no. The fog did clear from his eyes
enough for him to focus on me when he answered,
"Maybe so, maybe so," and ruffled my hair. I think
I'll spend the rest of my writing time on crocodiles.

Wed. Sept. 29

ENOUGH OF THIS! I'm tired of crocodiles,
tired of Mom not being bubbly; I <u>don't</u> want
Jesse's eggs and bacon again tomorrow and I
don't want to write about it!

Wednesday evening

I didn't think things could get weirder. I was wrong. After getting off the bus this afternoon, Jesse raced me to the mail, as usual, and beat me, as usual, and started flipping through it on the way to the house. I headed on up the drive, figuring he'd catch up as usual, but he didn't. Glancing back I saw him just standing in the middle of the road staring at the envelopes in his hand. The gravel crunching under my feet as I went back didn't snap him out of it, but reaching for the mail sure did. Snatching it out of my reach he shouted, "No! Just go home!" I was really taken back. "Jesse, what's wrong?"

"Nothing, - - - just - - - nothing. Leave me alone!" And he ran all the way back to the house.

When I got up there - no Jesse; just Mom and Dad standing in the kitchen with their arms around each other. Dad looked surprised to see me and said, "I didn't hear the bus. Where's Jesse?"

"I don't know," I told him and tossed my backpack down by the hall tree and went to look, pretending not to notice Mom hadn't looked at me, she just stepped away from Dad and went to the sink.

I hope they didn't have a fight. I couldn't see mom's eyes, but Dad's were kind of red and damp. There was no new wood split at the wood pile though.

I didn't go up to Jesse when I saw him out in the orchard just standing there, staring, but no longer vacant and far away. He was very much there but like a caged wild animal, frantic but frozen. Then his eyes changed, focused. I looked where he was looking; it was at Mom, walking towards him. He marched over to meet her. Stopping toe to toe, jaw set, eyes unwavering, he lifted an envelope up in front of her eyes. She looked at it, then back at him. Smiling gently she gave him a hug. I couldn't hear what she said, then they turned and headed towards the house. I picked up his backpack from where he'd dropped it and went on in.

Dinner conversation was fake and empty. I just wish I knew what was going on. Everyone is here in the house but it still feels vacant.

Dad just called us from the livingroom.

Maybe I don't want to know.

Jesse is at the door.

His eyes are big and dark.

He just reached out to me.

Thu.

NO!!! ANGRY ANGRY

ANGRY

ANGRY

ANGRY

Fri,

I HATE MY MOM

STUPID STUPID STUPID

STUPID

STUPID

I HATE HATE HATE HATE

HATE !

To thine own self be true

I love my Mom

My Mom has cancer.

Mon. October 4

Cancer (**kan**·sər) *n.* Any of a group of often fatal diseases characterized by abnormal cellular growth.

Tues. Oct. 5

Melanoma (**mel**·ə·**NŌ**·mə) *n.* A rapidly spreading, usually fatal form of skin cancer.

NOOOOOOOO!!!!

No No No!! WWWW

Fatal (**fāt**·əl) *adj.* Resulting in or capable of causing death.

Wed. 6

I'm so sick inside. I think I might throw up. Maybe I should go home. I mentioned that to Jesse at lunch but he snapped, "You're not the one that's sick! Knock it off!" Then he climbed over the back fence and spent the rest of lunch break stomping through the pasture, smacking at the tall grass with a stick.

Island.
An island in a sea of people, whispering, pointing. No one knows what to say. They just make furtive glances and keep their distance. Every time I catch Heather looking at me, she turns away fast, but not fast enough. I see her eyes fill up. Can't I go home?

Thursday 7
Halloween. We are all supposed to know what we're doing today. Kayleen, Kevin and Kyle are doing a reading of <u>The Legend of Sleepy Hollow</u>, Christopher and Nathan want to be scary trees for their background. C.C. is playing the piano.

Jesse was slumped down at his desk, concealed inside his faded navy-blue hoodie. Heather just shrugged. Jonathan muttered something about having an idea he was trying to figure out.

I figured I'd better say something and mentioned writing a poem but that I was having trouble starting. Mr. Moore said we'd go around the room and everyone would say some scary words and maybe some of them would help light a spark.

He pulled down on the roll of paper that hangs above the marker board and wrote what people called out. Wicked, blood, black cats, ghouls, goblins, vampires, werewolves, but nothing was clicking. My turn. Nothing – blank.

"Just one scary thing," Mr. Moore urged
"Melanoma."
I opened my mouth and it just spilled out.

A vacuum, sucking all the sound from the room. Mr. Moore drew a long raspy breath. "That's a scary one all right." Would anyone ever look at me?

Jonathan jumped up. "I know. That could be one of the games we play, stab the melanoma."
"Yeah," Heather agreed and jumped up to the

front of the class, grabbed a big brown marker, and made a giant, blobby shape around the words Mr. Moore had written. "We could throw darts at it," Nathan cried. C.C. suggested making cardboard daggers to stab it with. "Forget cardboard," cried Gibb, "Let's really stab it." He started for the scissors. Mr. Moore stopped Gibb with a raised hand, but not the rising energy.

Everyone charged the board and tore down the paper. "Kill the beast," Heather shouted and we all started shredding it. Any minute Mr. Moore would stop it I knew.

But he didn't. A frenzy of paper shreds filled the air. We stared at the littered floor as the last fragment floated down. But only for a moment. "Burn the beast," was the next shout.

Arms scooped and pushed the sheds into the trashcan, which was handed to me. We all marched out to the burn barrel. Mr. Moore ceremoniously handed a match to Jesse who struck it and dropped it in.

Which was more satisfying - the fire or how everyone joined in - or the way people looked at Jesse and me and talked to us directly? Heather's hand slipped into mine as the flames died down. Mr. Moore said we could take an early lunch break, so we just stayed outside.

The ridge beyond the playground is so beautiful and peaceful with bright yellow maple trees tucked into all the green firs with a touch of red here and there. It was good to be out in the fresh air.

Friday Oct 8th

It's cloudy in town. I didn't feel like swimming today so I told the swim teacher I thought I was getting a cold. "You do look a little under the weather," she agreed. "Why don't you sit out today."

From the bleachers everyone looked so far away. Cold echoes of splashes bounced off the walls in another world. Not until someone walked up to me did I realize I had floated off somewhere and everyone had gone to the shower rooms. I looked up. It was Jonathan. Hmm. Guess he didn't race to get a hot shower for once.

He looked down at his feet. "You write really good poetry, Amy. I was wondering," he paused and started to put his hands in his pockets but there weren't any pockets. "I had an idea for Halloween but couldn't work it out and you'd do a lot better anyway." He glanced over his shoulder at the boy's door, at me, back at his feet, then took a deep breath and plunged ahead. "You know the three witch's thing in <u>MacBeth</u>?"

"Bubble, bubble, toil and trouble?" I asked.

He glanced up, "Yeah," and back down. "Well, what about re-writing it, maybe into something funny?"

"Who would be the three witches," I wondered.

He finally raised his eyes, "You, me and Heather?" He looked hopeful.

My first instinct was to say no, but then I agreed to talk to Heather. I told her on the way home and she shrieked with laughter, "You have GOT to be kidding!" I saw Jonathan several seats ahead of us shrink down and his neck got all red. It didn't make me feel good. So I got out my journal. If I'm writing people leave me alone. Mr. Moore rode to town with us today so I'll give him this when I get off the bus.

Monday,   October 11th

Heather and I talked over the weekend. She remembered that Jonathan <u>used</u> to be fun, before he turned into such a pain last year. She's right. He used to make me laugh. And since we haven't been able to come up with an idea for the program, what the heck. If he's still awful to work with, we can ditch him.

When Mr. Moore gave me back my journal this morning, there was a note on it asking when would be a good time for me to talk to him for a minute. Probably about some of my 'writing' last week. Tough.

Tues. Oct. 12th

It didn't have anything to do with *how* I'd written, only *what* I'd written.

"Amy, the dictionaries here are pretty old and medical science changes really fast," he told me. "Cancer is not always the death sentence it was years ago. If caught early, ANY cancer can be stopped." Then he reminded me about Ms. Pascalla. She was treated for cancer just two years ago and is perfectly OK. In fact, she's so OK that I'd forgotten all about it! I bet I was getting all worked up over nothing. Mom would NEVER be so careless as to let something happen to her. What a huge weight off my stomach. I know people usually say mind, but my stomach felt it even more. A big millstone was plopped on my middle and wouldn't let me eat but now it's gone.

I curled up on Mom's lap last night and we talked and talked. She reminded me of our friend, Ken, who had cancer and chemotherapy and he hasn't had a trace of it for 7 years. He's fine. So are Jane and Maggie and a couple of other people that I didn't even know had had it.

Dr. Long said the melanoma was very, very small and he was sure he had gotten it all. They will know for sure when they get the test results back. Mom laughed when she said, "And I thought it was tough waiting to get a test back in college!" She had expected to hear by now but, "no news is good news."

Wed. Oct. 13th

I couldn't believe Jonathan was so jazzed when Heather and I said we'd give it a try. "Rad!" he exclaimed and brought a copy of <u>MacBeth</u> today. We actually had a lot of fun reading the three witches' parts.

> Round about the cauldron go
> In the poisoned entrails throw,
> Toad that under coldest stone
> Days and night hast 31,
> Sweltered venom, sleeping got
> Boil thou 1st in the charmed pot.
>   Double double, toil and trouble;
>   Fire burn and cauldron bubble
> Fillet of fenny snake,
> In the cauldron boil and bake,
> Eye of newt and toe of frog
> Wool of bat and tongue of dog,
> Adder's fork & blind worm's sting
> Lizard's leg and owlet's wing,
> For a charm of powerful trouble
> Like a hell-broth, boil & bubble.

Double double, toil and trouble;
Fire burn and cauldron bubble.
Scale of dragon, tooth of wolf
Witches' mummy, maw and gulf
Of the raven'd salt-sea shark
Root of Hemlock, digged in dark,
Make the gruel thick and slab
Pitch delivered by a drab,
Add there to a tiger's chaudron
For the ingredients of our cauldron.
Double double, toil and trouble;
Fire burn and cauldron bubble.
Cool it with a baboon's blood
Then the charm is firm and good,
Thrice the blinded cat hath mewed
Thrice and once the hedge pig whined,
Harper cries – 'Tis time, 'tis time.

Now to re-write it.

Mom is having her stitches out today and is sure Dr. Long will have the test results. She's positive it's OK but agrees it'll be nice to have it official.

Thurs. Oct. 14

"No news is good news." What a stupid saying.
What an incredibly stupid, *stupid, STUPID* saying.
IT SUCKS! I don't want to be here. I don't want
to feel this and I *don't* want to write about it*!*

Fri
AAAAGH!!!

Black, black, sinking, swirling, falling, falling,
endless hole.   Spinning - can't stop.
Sharp knives;   my eyes, my head, my heart-
        stabbing, stabbing,

                falling,
                    so dark

45

Mon. Oct. 18th

Now we wait. Mom's going to need another operation. The melanoma was bigger than they thought at first and now more skin tissue needs to be taken and checked to be safe. Dr. Long could do that but he also wants a Lymphadenectomy. That's not even in the dictionary but Mom explained it to us. They will inject radio-active dye where the melanoma was and track it to the first lymph-node it goes to. Removing and testing it will show if the cancer has spread. If it's clear, that's the end of it. Please let that be the end of it.

Tues. Oct. 19th

I sat and re-read the last couple of weeks. I can't believe it was just a month ago Mom came back with a little band-aide on her chest. I was so oblivious [(ob·liv·e·us) *adj.* Not conscious or aware.] Wish I still was.

Wed, Oct. 20th

It's good to have something else to think about. Changing the witches' speech is harder than we thought. It's so good the way it is. We'd just about decided to read it the way it's written, but inspiration finally arrived. We're trying to set it in school and might use 'microwave' instead of 'cauldron.'

Thurs. Oct. 21st

Chicken lips, frog tails, shark's nose tip, slug slime trail.

We are just working on things we might use and rhyming them. We'll work on it tomorrow too, on the way to town. We are going to see a play. It'll be great.

Mon. Oct. 25th

YEA! It's almost Halloween. The air is sooo crisp out each morning. Mom helped us get our costumes together this weekend. A surprise in the mail Friday really helped. I guess Mom told Aunt Joan what we were doing because she'd sewn three matching witch hats and sent them. They're great. Aunt Joan can do <u>anything</u>.

Mom got out a black cape she'd used for a bat costume once and surprised me with a black skirt from the thrift store. I found a foot long plastic skeleton that I won last year and I'm going to hang it from a belt around my waist. "Too rad," Jonathan said when I told him and he decided to hang a bat from his belt. He's not coming as a boy witch. We all wanted to kind of look alike so he's going to wear a skirt too. A lot of guys wouldn't do that but he's cool.

Jesse's going to be a hunchback but he won't let us see it. Heather said everyone would recognize him anyway since he's sure to have his raggedy old hoodie on. I don't know though. He found an old, equally faded brown hooded cape, then cloistered himself away in his room.

[Cloistered (**klois**·stəred) *adv.* Concealed or withdrawn from the world.]

It's going to be a good costume though, I could hear him chuckling and snorting to himself in there, making odd clumping and snuffling sounds.

Mom and Dad are going to be scarecrows and do apples-on-a-string for our contribution to the games. We did bobbing-for-apples last year, but people's make-up came off in the water. The black and green was slimy enough, but when the red from Bozo's nose ran, it was down-right putrid. Sophie was sure they were poisoned apples. YEEESHH!

Our family carved our pumpkins Sunday. They grew really well this year. Jesse and I claimed ours in August, and Dad helped us put straw under them so they could finish growing without sitting in the dirt and roly-poly bugs. Jesse's is really fierce looking. I tried to make mine fierce but it just looks cute. The one tooth on the bottom makes it look like a happy baby. Mom drew hers out but Dad cut it.

She sighed, "I don't even think about the incision unless I push hard, or try to carry something heavy. Then it gives me a sharp reminder." ☺

Tues. Oct. 26th

Round about the classroom go
In the naughty students throw,
Toad that under coldest sink
Sits with golden eyes that wink,
Hold it up until it wets
Then mix it with some piggy sweat,
Blow a nose for slimy snot
Boil it in the chamber pot.
　　Double double, boil and bubble,
　　Give the students toil and trouble.
Fill the pot and give a shake

In microwave, let boil and bake.

Eye of newt, toe of dog

Fur of snake and scale of frog

Adder's kiss and wormy's wing,

Make the collared lizard sing

Chicken lips, bullfrog tails,

Turkey hooves, slug slime trails.
　　Double double, boil and bubble,
　　Give the students toil and trouble.
Cook with grits, stir and putter
Then melt in a slab of butter.
No, no! That cannot be,
Who turned the page of the recipe?
Crush up one small snake hip-bone

Now throw in a musty crone.
Oh that's me, that will not do,
What will make this thick as goo?
Boil some more and let me think,
Ah, throw in the kitchen sink.
For a charm of powerful trouble
Throw the students in to bubble.
    Now our frightening brew is done
    and all of you had better run!
AAAAGH!!!

All of our herpetology reports are done and
hanging on the bulletin board. My croc is
beauteous with big shiny teeth. We named
Jonathan's salamander Gracie Gracie, and made
her a nice cage label.

Wed. Oct. 27th

Today everyone performed for each other in
the center room and we will every day the rest of
the week. It's good practice for the performers
and for the little kids to learn how to sit quietly.
Last Friday was a sore reminder that people don't
automatically know how to be a good audience.

Since show and tell in kindergarten, we've heard, "Sit still. Don't talk. Keep your hands *and* feet to yourself. It's so-and-so's turn, so be a good audience."

At the play we went to Friday there was a class seated in front of us who had *not* been taught that. They were big kids too, older than me even. "Haven't they ever been allowed out in public before?" I heard Kayleen mutter. Some of them kept talking, OUT LOUD even, *during* the show, giggling and scuffling.

Our whole school almost laughed out loud when little E.S. leaned forward and shushed them. It finally got better when a teacher took two of the boys out. She must have been soooo humiliated. [Humiliate (hyoo·**mil**·e·āt) Subject to feelings of inferiority, worthlessness, to mortify.]

Thurs. Oct. 28th

Mom's been coming all week to help Mrs. Mitchell with the little kids. Mrs. Donaldson came today too. Ron was new this year. His brother Roy is a year younger, and came with his mom too. What a crack-up. He calls Ron, Ronald McDonald. Together they are a couple of fireballs. Mrs. Donaldson said she almost felt guilty sending them both to Mrs. Mitchell's class next year. They were *not* good audience members until their mom took Roy to the back row and he sat on her lap.

This morning Mr. Goodwin had the 7th and 8th graders help him set up chairs and the platform for the stage. Everyone is supposed to bring their costumes for the rehearsal tomorrow. It's one thing to practice in everyday clothes and quite another when you suddenly have tails and wings and wands getting in the way. It's better to nip the problems in the bud beforehand.

Last year, when the 'M' class kids were in 1st grade, they all had crowns for one part. When they bowed, the crowns all fell off and rolled off the stage, clunking on the floor. Marie and May were totally flustered. Monte laughed so hard he fell on the floor. Ever sensible Mark just hopped down and picked them up. Ms. Pascalla stapled on elastic to go under their chins and everything went just fine that night.

Tonight I promised to help Mom braid her hair. She still can't raise her arm enough to do much. I'm going to make her lots and lots of little braids then get them wet so when I unbraid them tomorrow night, her hair will be all kinky. She thought it would be a good look for my witchy hair too, so she's going to braid my hair when I'm done.

Friday, October 29th

I LOVE HALLOWEEN. Everybody looked so rad this morning. The Abernathys and Abercrombies are all going to be swamp snakes in honor of our herpetology studies. Turns out, they've spent weeks gathering algae and drying it and collecting the pale green moss that hangs from trees. Their ghoul sheets got dyed a murky green and long strings of moss and algae covered them, even hanging down over their faces. Mommy 'A' found a batch of rubber snake noses with elastic bands to hold them on. When they wear them the noses stick out of the stringy mossy strands which hang

over their faces and they all look truly snakey.
It's the best Aberration's group yet. Absolutely.
Punny, punny, ha ha.

Heather has a witch nose on elastic, like the
snake noses, so for our witch performance she'll
just switch noses and voila', she's the best witch
of all - although Jonathan really looks great too.

I thought he might get teased but only Jordon
and Ron even attempted it. They whistled at him
but he just turned around and made a sexy pose.
"Hey boys," he blew them a loud smacky kiss, and
everyone just rolled. I never knew he could be so
hilarious.

The biggest costume problem was for the 3rd,
4th and 5th grade girls. Shereese, Kitty, D.D. and
Anna have all worked out a great dance to <u>Monster
Mash</u>. The first part went fine but when they
twirled to the right, Anna and Kitty's moss swirled
around and got caught on each other's and when
they twirled back left, Anna stepped on Shereese's
cat tail and D.D.'s wand smacked Kitty in the face.
Luckily Kitty had her rubber snake nose on and only
dented it temporarily.

So, no wand during the dance, the tail needs to be shorter and Anna and Kitty can't stand next to each other.

Christopher and Nathan had to move way apart too, so their limbs wouldn't tangle. They did get to be trees for <u>The Legend of Sleepy Hollow</u>, but they had to be narrators. Mr. Moore wouldn't let them just stand there.

Jordan and Ron gave every one a good laugh. They both came as red-haired clowns. "Will the *real* Ronald McDonald please stand up?" That's what Roy said.

Mrs. Donaldson asked if the adults dressed up too. "Oh absolutely," grinned Mom. "Otherwise everyone points and snickers." They don't, of course, but everyone really gets into the spirit around here. People live really spread out in this countryside; some are pretty isolated and everyone jumps at the chance for a little socializing and they "come out with bells on," as Mom would say.

Dad came over last night to help set up the Haunted House in the storage barn. The dads really go all out and do their best to scare people.

Anyone can go in, but the little kids always seem to melt out of line when screams issue forth from the barn.

Heather never has made it. She got clear in the door last year but when a real skeleton hand fell forward and grabbed her, she was gone and my ears were ringing from her scream.

"Do *NOT* let me run this year," she begged me. "Tie me to you if you have to."

Then D.D. said, "Don't feel bad, C.C. and I haven't made it yet either." (I didn't know that.) She added, "Thought I could do it last year, but that skeleton got to me too."

"It got better after that," I told them. "Just go with a group and don't be first or last. They get grabbed the most. Jesse told me that."

Heather whacked me with her rubber nose. "So that's why you were behind me!"

She wasn't really mad though. This is going to be sooo great. "Rad," Jonathan says, "Rad."

Mon. November 1st

Bummer. Deflated like the balloons and saggy, draggy crepe paper hanging limp from the moisture collected over the weekend. I can see Mr. Goodwin on a ladder in the next room, taking it all down. But Friday night - it was all we could have hoped for. Hairy, scary, merry, nary a carey. Ha, ha.

Mom and Dad were great scarecrows with hay sticking out of their sleeves and pant legs.

Jesse was awesome and awful. He surprised us all with some glued on face pieces and fake drool, making snorting, slobbering sounds as he lurched around dragging one foot. He and Gibb did a great presentation of <u>Jabberwocky</u>. It was my favorite. After ours. ☺ Everyone loved the three witches!

<u>The Legend of Sleepy Hollow</u>, turned out well but Christopher and Nathan took their limbs off right after it because they were poking everyone. No-one's costumes got torn up in the <u>Monster Mash</u>.

Of course the littlest kids stole the show, as always. Mrs. Mitchell read a story and they each had a picture to hold up when she said the word -

tree, moon, cat, etc. They were sooo cute standing
there as elves, clowns, fairies and Elvis, taking it
all so seriously. Inevitably some were late with
their pictures, too busy smiling at parents, and
their neighbor had to nudge them. Some ended up
with their pictures upside-down. I did, when I was
in kindergarten. Thought everyone was just
giggling because I was so cute. Guess I was. What
happened, huh?

Anyway, the kindergarteners have done the
same thing every year for forever and ever and
everyone always loves it. After the program, the
Haunted House was opened and the games started.
YEA!

Apples on a string – big hit. Mom had three
baskets of different sized apples for different
sized mouths. Hands were supposed to be kept
behind backs but if really small kids were getting
frustrated, Mom would look away just long enough
for a little hand to slip up and help out.

E.S. was such a smarty - he patiently used his
mouth to carry his apple up and over the rod it was
tied to, again and again until the apple was tight
against the rod. Then he bit it. Mom laughed and
laughed. "You will go far in this world," she told

him. But then she re-tied the strings loose around the rod so no one else could do that. Monte tried and tried. He must have taken it over the rod for 10 minutes before he realized it wasn't winding up. I am *not* saying how long it took me to get mine.

Jonathan did the best. He got it swinging so hard that he just opened his mouth wide and it swung back and smacked him hard enough to stick on his teeth. Heather and I literally rolled on the floor and Mom laughed so hard her straw started falling out.

The Haunted House? SUCCESS! ! Kitty and Anna were going to go with Heather, Jonathan and I, but when the vampire guide came for the group in front of us, he lunged at Shereese, catching her off guard. She fled, shrieking, Kitty and Anna too.

Heather jumped a bit and looked after them longingly, but Jonathan and I grabbed her from each side. "Uh uh uhh," I told her and we didn't let go until we were coming out. Then I lost it, I must confess. I was expecting the dead guys in the coffins to sit up and grab at us, but I thought they were the last and started to breathe easier then was caught off guard by a cold slimy thing slithering fast around my ankles. AAHHH!! I must have leap-frogged or something because suddenly I was outside and gone and Heather and Jonathan were still in the doorway.

"What? What?" they asked when they caught up, but I just collapsed on the ground laughing. It was the best.

Tues. Nov. 2nd

What is WRONG with me?

Yesterday the world seemed fine and bright. But now I'm reminded that it's hollow and fragile. Yesterday was a nice smooth road, now all I see is a bog with mud and quicksand. Mom and Dad are leaving Sunday. How could I forget? Two weeks ago it seemed a long way away; next month. How could I have laughed and played and been so light-hearted?!

[Betrayal – (bi·**trā**·al) *n.* To prove faithless; to deceive and desert.] I should have had her on my mind all the time, to support her and help her some way. I don't know how - just - just by making it so in my mind. Dad said how Jesus could walk on water by believing he could. I will <u>believe</u> she will be alright. I will believe it so hard it will make it so.

Wed. Nov 3rd

I'm all hollow and woosie inside. I look at my
work and it just swirls around on the page. I
couldn't eat lunch. I feel empty but not hungry.
I think eating would be a bad idea.

Th. Nov. 4th

It's gray out. Gray in. No color, like the
beginning of the <u>Wizard of Oz</u>; all the color
sucked away.

Mom's been here every day for nearly two
weeks. "Sitting at home makes the day too long,"
She told Mrs. Olsen. I guess waiting is hard for
her too.

Stupid me, of course it is. It's her life. I've
only thought about ME if she were gone, not Jesse,
not Dad and definitely not her. Is she afraid?
Afraid she won't see us grow up? Does she wonder
if she will get to hold her grandchildren and grow
old with Dad? If she doesn't, would Dad remarry?
I don't even want to think about that*!*

Maybe she thinks we would stop hurting after awhile and life would go on like normal, just like before Halloween when I forgot to worry. The sun would come up and we'd laugh and play and try to get on, but she would be gone and not be a part of it. Our friend Louise that died, I hardly ever think of her. She was important when she was in our life, but it's been so long. I think of her and try to feel something, anything, even the pain that used to come when I wanted to go see her and remembered sharply that I couldn't. Nothing comes but anger. Anger at myself for betraying someone who cared about me. It should Hurt! If Mom goes, will I betray her too? It should hurt every day of my life. It hurts now.

The paper's all blurry; head aches. I'll rest my eyes a bit.

Fri. N. 5

OH My Goodness!
We have an hour before we go to town. We're seeing a magician before we swim. I have some spelling to study but I'll write fast. I have so much to say.

Dad wasn't home yet when we got off the bus. "He needed to do some shopping," Mom told us as she fixed dinner. It was cloudy and dark when we heard him drive in. "Better go help with the groceries," she urged us. I dragged my feet putting on my coat. The book I was reading was good and I wasn't interested in heavy grocery bags.

Then I heard Jesse shout. Mr. Cool, Calm and Collected? And it wasn't a 'Wow, what good food,' shout. Rushing out to see what was up, I realized there were <u>four</u> people – AAAHHH ! <u>Five</u>, as I threw myself at them!

It was Grandma and Grandpa Blair! I couldn't believe it! We only see them about once a year. "Well it's about time." Mom stepped out smiling and drying her hands on her apron.

Hugs and kisses and, "It's so good to see you's," were passed around. I caught them scrutinizing Mom when her eyes were turned away. I knew they were searching for some visual sign. I could have told them, 'Don't bother.' Nothing shows in her walk or talk or smile. Only when she thinks no one is around, then you might see it in the way she sits so very still and gazes far away. But not tonight. It was bubbles and smiles and laughs. What a good day.

Monday, November 8th

Tick – tick - tick. I hear each time the skinny clock hand clicks forward. A new second, one more gone. It's 1:00. They would be finishing lunch and heading for the 1:30 doctor's appointment. A lavender note in my pocket carries their schedule. I wanted it, to keep track of what's happening. Jesse asked, "Why?" and looked at me like I was nuts. He does that a lot lately.

Mom understood though. She'd already written everything down on the back of the doctor's card. They are at the hospital now. That hospital. Not our hospital; where I was born; where they gave me five stitches and set Jesse's broken arm. "Why not?" I complained. "Why go all the way to San Francisco?"

Jesse gave me that, 'You are hopelessly stupid,' look. "You want her to have the best, don't you?" Now <u>that</u> was a stupid question.

Mom was more patient. "The Lymphadenectomy procedure is still pretty new and Dr. Long really thought it was necessary. I want to do everything I can . . ." she trailed off for a moment. "So I'm going." And they did.

Yesterday morning she came into my room and gave me a long hug before kissing me good-bye. Then she went into Jesse's room. Would he want a long hug too? Does he think he's too big?

When the front door clicked closed behind her I pushed the curtain away from my window and looked down on the driveway. She came into sight then stopped and turned back. Had she forgotten something? No, she just closed her eyes a couple of moments, then stepped out of the porch light and went on, leaving footprints on the frosty ground. I stayed, listening to the tires crunch on the gravel. The car stopped down at the gate then continued on, growing fainter and fainter 'til I realized it was only the wind I was hearing. A shiver ran down me. I hadn't put on my robe.

I tippy-toed down the hall, the wooden floor cold and hard on my bare feet. Light from the kitchen spilled across the shadowy living room. Grandma jumped a little when I stepped into the kitchen. The steam rising from her flowered teacup, had fogged her glasses. They cleared as she set the cup down on the table. "Didn't realize you'd climbed out of your warm, cozy bed." Then she looked passed me. "You too?" I hadn't heard

Jesse behind me. "Wouldn't you two be better off getting another hour's sleep?" We just stood, silently. "Guess you probably wouldn't sleep anyway. Why don't you go let your Grandpa know he doesn't have to tippy-toe around anymore and we'll have breakfast."

Now I'm tired though. 1:49. Mom and Dad are talking to the doctor now.

Tues. 9th

They should be all done with the radio-active dye and starting to get ready for surgery. It scares me that she will be totally unconscious this time.

Before, with Dr. Long, it was only a local anesthesia. I asked her if she had gotten grossed out.

"No, I thought I might, but I didn't. I am pretty squeamish about such things and can't even watch when I give blood, but I didn't feel woozy until afterwards when I was checking out. Then I had to sit down while your Dad finished the paperwork."

I'm the same way. Whenever there's anything medical shown on the news, I have to look away and plug my ears. The news guy might think it's great to show brain scans or a heart pumping away in a pool of blood but I'll pass, thank you very much. Even when Jesse was describing how the doctor set his broken arm, I passed out.

So when I finally got up the courage to ask Mom about the details of her last surgery, part of me REALLY didn't want to know, but part of me did. I needed to, as if by sharing the knowledge, I could share her burden.

"Did they mask off your chest, or could you see what they were doing?"

"Oh, I could have seen had I cared to," she chuckled. "But you can be sure I didn't look. I was glad to be doing as well as I was and I certainly wasn't going to push it. I could hear everything though," she continued. The weirdest part was when they cauterized the blood vessels. I could hear the sizzles and see smoke rising from my chest, but I could feel absolutely nothing."

That was quite enough information for <u>me</u> on the subject.

[Cauterize (**KAW**·tər·īz) v. The destruction of tissue by searing.]

Wed. Nov. 10th

She called last night. I'd gone to bed but was just lying there, looking at the ceiling. When Grandpa answered the phone I could tell by his voice who it was and bounded down the hall. I was fast but Jesse was faster. Grandpa switched on the speakerphone, "So you don't have to repeat yourself four times."

The surgery had gone well but she was really tired. They were staying in a hotel in the city and will probably be home tomorrow night. - Tonight. I wanted to know more, but Grandma said she should get some rest.

I REALLY wanted to talk more. Actually I guess what I wanted was just to hear her voice, maybe to sing me to sleep, all curled up in her lap. I wanted to hear that everything was fine and there were no more worries.

Grandma seemed to know what was whirling around inside me. "You can't have your cake and eat it too." What a stupid saying. What's the point of having cake if you can't eat it? She came to tuck me in though, and sang softly to me. They were nice songs, but they weren't Mom's songs.

It's 1:30. They're out there somewhere on the road now. Driving – driving. Drive safe. What if they were to have an accident? What if she made it through surgery only to die in a fiery crash?

KNOCK IT OFF! Jesse would call that, "wallowing," pulling down bad feelings all around myself and wallowing in them like a pig in mud. They are just fine!

Friday, Nov. 12th

Yesterday was Veteran's Day so no school. We got to spend the whole day home with Mom. She hadn't planned it that way she said, but it certainly worked out well.

After we got home from school Wed. I picked a bouquet from what was left after the frost. It didn't look like enough so I went up on the hill and got stems of dark orange berries. On the way back I found some ferns that still looked good. After I got them all arranged nicely I started watching the clock, wondering where they might be. I'd run to the window every time I heard a car or truck on the road. Grandpa said I needn't bother, that they probably wouldn't be home before we were in bed. But they were! Even with all my watching though, I missed them driving up.

The cornbread, ham and beans were all ready and I was setting the table; dishes clacking and silverware clashing covered any other sound until I heard Jesse clumping down the stairs, two at a time - flying along, then he suddenly slowed, trying to act nonchalant,

[(**non·**shə·**LANT**) *n.* exhibiting a casual lack interest or excitement.]

I didn't though. Rushing passed, I threw myself at them. Dad swooped me up. "Ho there, Amy girl! You're not glad to see us are you?"

Mom got out of the car kind of stiff and slow but with a big smile. "Hey Amy." She hugged me with her left arm. "You too, mister all-grown-up." She motioned Jesse over. He hugged her like she might break. So did Grandma and Grandpa who were very teary eyed.

Dinner was warm and wonderful and our house felt whole again. Mom sighed like I do when sinking down in a hot bubble bath, and made yummy noises over the beans and cornbread. All was perfect until Jesse asked when she would know the results of the Lymphadenectomy.

"In about two weeks," she answered.

TWO WEEKS! Why does everything have to be two weeks? Why can't they just do the test or whatever they do, right then? It was hard enough waiting for the surgery, now Two Weeks?!

Mon. Nov. 15th

The bandage is bigger than I expected. Jesse glowered at me when I reached over and touched the white puffy edge that was poking up at the neck of her shirt. She said the incision isn't that big, they just wanted to give it lots of protection. I have so many questions but I haven't gotten to talk to her much. She sleeps an awful lot. Reminds me of my cousin, Cindy, when she was a little baby. I was so looking forward to playing with Cindy on our first visit but she slept almost the entire time.

Mom doesn't sleep <u>that</u> much but I am ready to have everything back to normal, and it's not.

"Sleeping is a good thing," Grandma told me. "It will help her heal faster." So Mom must be healing really fast then.

She did get up early the first morning back, to start breakfast. "What do you think YOU'RE doing?" Grandma scolded. "I came here to help take care of you. Now you're going to let me, aren't you?"

Mom laughed, "I guess I can handle that," and laid down until breakfast. After school she sits on the couch long enough to hear what Jesse and I have been doing, but then lies back down.

I remember after her first surgery, she held her right arm tight against her side for awhile. She's doing that again, only more so; shoulder stiff and high, elbow tucked tight, and arm held like it's in a sling. She looks deformed.

When I asked her why she held it like that, Jesse shot me a really nasty look. What? Was I supposed to pretend that was normal?

Mom answered cheerfully, "The skin is stretched so tightly across my chest, it feels like it could tear if I move anything."

I stuck my tongue out at Jesse. It was <u>not</u> a stupid question, so there!

Tues. Nov. 16th

I don't think Mom will be in to help at school for awhile. She gets up so slowly. First the right hand goes to her chest, then she slowly pushes herself up-right with her left, and sits a moment before slowly standing. She saw me watching, and with a smile, answered my look. "I never really appreciated the force of gravity before. No wonder we sag and wrinkle over time. I'm just surprised it doesn't happen even faster. It feels like I've got an old flat iron strapped to my chest whenever I move."

When she was out of sight I got a shove from behind. "Knock it off," Jesse hissed.

ME! He's the one that needs to knock it off. What is his problem?

Anyway, she went to bed early and it was really strange not having her around while I was doing my homework. Dad helped me with a math problem and Grandpa read me my spelling words, the regular ones and some new harder ones he found to keep me on my "competition toes." I got everything done OK, it was just weird.

Wed. Nov. 17th

Mom was sleeping when we came home yesterday. She was lying on her back and her shirt sagged across her chest. She seems thinner. Maybe not - maybe it's just the way that fat bandage sticks up and makes her look different. I hate it. I want it gone. I want Mom to feel like she used to when I hug her. And I want Jesse to be like Jesse again. He saw me standing in the doorway and with a glower he motioned me away with a jerk of his head like some self-appointed guard dog.

Thurs. Nov. 18th

Grandma helped Mom take a bath again last night. She has to keep her bandages from getting wet, plus she can't raise her arm to wash her hair. When it was dry, I combed it out, I know just how, after years of her combing my long hair. Dad tried once, but he started at the top and made a mess of it. So I comb it every day now. I braided it too, I thought it was kind of messy and uneven but she just squeezed me tight with her left arm and said, "Thanks sooo much Amy, my little hair dresser." Then she laid on the couch with her head in my lap while I read my reading assignment out loud.

Friday, Nov. 19th

That was fun. The little kids all have beautiful pinecone turkeys to take home. The upper class, (of which I am now a part) helped them. Each of us worked with one student. I got the kindergartener, Zoë.

She was so cute, all frowning in concentration and her upper lip pulled down by her teeth as she cut out her colored paper feathers. She got a little heavy with the paste and didn't wipe her hands so when she tucked her hair behind her ears she slid clumps of paste through the strands. I tried to wipe the worst of it out.

I had it easy. Jesse got Mark from the 'M' class.

They are all second graders now and pretty easy on the art part but very challenging on the behavior end.

Now with all of us in there helping, Mrs. Mitchell stepped in to the office briefly, just briefly, she said.

All was fine - - - for a whole moment, until Mark got up for a drink and everyone saw two paper feathers glued to his rear.

Monte gave himself away, taking a quick peek as soon as Mark stood up, then clasping his hands over his mouth in an attempt to conceal his mirth which bubbled out anyway and rolled him onto the floor.

When Mark turned around and saw Monte laughing on the floor he asked, "What?" accusingly and all the other 'M's lost it.

Jesse got up to peel the feathers off, but Mark, oblivious to his attempted help, started turning in a circle to try and see behind himself.

Jesse tried to get behind him but whichever

way he went, Mark would turn the other way and
then back again in a ridiculous dance routine until
C.C. said, "Mark, stand still."

Unfortunately Mark stopped while facing the
table, and suddenly with one frustrated sweep of
his arm, all the paper feathers went flying. Splat,
one with paste on it hit Marie on the arm and
stuck.

"Eew!" She flung it off – onto Monte's face as
he rolled on the floor. That got Mark laughing, but
only for a moment. Monte pulled himself up,
swooped the end of a feather through some paste
and gave it a fling. Splat, it stuck to Mark's chest.
At our table, Ronald McDonald jumped up with a
hand full of feathers and a loaded paste stick.

Jonathan grabbed him by the collar so fast his
feet spun under him like a cartoon character on
ice.   "Don't even think it," Jonathan ordered.

The whole thing took less than a minute, then
Mrs. Mitchell popped back in the door and all was
in order again and we were able to finish the VERY
cute turkeys.

Mon. Nov. 22nd

We are supposed to be working on
Thanksgiving poems. Thankful –Thankful –
what rhymes? Hankful, dankful, sankful.
It eludes me.
[(i·**lood**) *v.* To avoid or escape; evade.]

Tuesday 23rd

Oh my goossh! I can't believe Kevin.

The upper class always prepares the turkey
and dressing but a lot of them really don't have
a clue about cooking. It won't actually be baked
until tomorrow but we needed to get everything
ready today so Ms. Pascalla can pop it in the oven
early in the morning. It will fill the school with
marvelous smells as it cooks.

Well, Kevin got done with math early and Mr.
Moore said he could go see if Ms. Pascalla could
use any help yet.

When the rest of us were done and trooped into the kitchen, there was an outburst from the front of the group; "EEEWWW!" and C.C. dashed back out the door, followed by cries of, "Kevin! What are you doing?!" and great guffaws and cackling.

By the time I could make my way in enough to see, C.C. was coming back towing Ms. Pascalla. She suppressed a smile and hushed everyone.

"Well Kevin," she said gently as he stood there big eyed and puzzled with one arm submerged elbow deep in a sink of bubbles, the other hand poised with a scrub brush. "Thank you for such a thorough job. Although the next time you want to wash a turkey, just a rinse with straight water will do." He looked sheepishly at Mr. Turkey Lurky, floating in his bubble bath. "No harm done," she smiled. "We'll just rinse it off really well and have the cleanest bird in the county."

Mom sent a bag of fresh herbs. Ms. Pascalla made a point of commenting on all the wonderful smells she was responsible for but that only made it more obvious that she wasn't here this time.

Wednesday

She came! She came!
Suddenly I could write my poem.

The sun rises and I notice – sometimes.
The sun sets and I notice – sometimes.
And everything in between
Sometimes goes unseen,
From a tree leaf changing with time
To a friend's hand in mine;
A laugh, a tear, the songs I hear;
From the birds and trees,
From the earth and seas.
And sometimes I forget
      what my loved ones mean to me,
And that I should always treasure
      every memory.
But sometimes I remember
      that my life is beautiful;
Over flowing with joy and love,
      and for that, I am truly thankful.

P.S. We drew our Secret Santa names for Christmas. I got C.C. - Hmmm. What would an 8th grade girl like? I don't want her to think I'm childish.

Monday, Nov. 29th

Thanksgiving was great but it seems like such a long time ago. How am I supposed to concentrate? The math numbers just seem to float around on the page in a meaningless jumble. The only ones that make sense are the ones on the clock. They stand unflinching as the second-hand clicks along relentless in its even tick-tick-tick. Has the doctor called yet? Mom was hoping to hear Wednesday, but she wasn't surprised not to. Surely today. It has to be today. We could start into the Christmas season with the best gift of all.

Tues. 30

No. we won't

Wed. December 1st

Dad says they probably knew last Wednesday
but didn't want to ruin our holiday. What – do they
really think it will hurt less a few days later?

STUPID *STUPID* **STUPID** ~~FRECKING~~ *PEOPLE!!*

Mon. Dec. 6

I overheard Mom talking to Dad last night after everyone was in bed.

"I thought Sue Pascalla was being a little extreme, having Radiation after her cancer operation two years ago. The doctors were 98% sure they had gotten it all with surgery and it might never show up again, but if she chose to have Radiation, they would be 100% sure. Now I understand. Nothing is too extreme. I will do whatever it takes. No hesitation. No second thoughts. I will do anything and everything possible to insure staying here with you `and watching our children grow up." She paused before continuing. "I wish they hadn't found out; wish we could have protected them from the distress."

"I know," Dad answered, "but they'll be OK."

Yes we will be.

Tues. Dec. 7

Chemotherapy (kēm·o·THAIR·ə·pē) *n.* The treatment of diseases through the use of chemically synthesized drugs having a specific action against certain micro-organisms.

Wed. 8

She say's maybe her hair won't fall out. It would be sooo awful if it did. I can't imagine her anyway else but with long, thick hair. I've always loved how people turn and look at her as she walks down the street, all admiring. She never seems to notice, but I do. It makes me warm and smiley inside.

At least nothing is going to happen immediately. There was a long debate between Mom, Dad and Dr. Long. Mom was for starting immediately, but they are going to wait until after Christmas.

Christmas, what the heck am I going to get C.C.? Why couldn't I have drawn Heather?

Th Dec 9

Only 8 days until Christmas break. I am ready for a break. I think everyone is. We've been working on our Winter Program but I'm having a hard time getting into it. I'm afraid there just isn't going to be a creative contribution from Amy Dixon this year. No poem, no story. Words are not my friends these days. They just ramble around in there aimlessly, pointlessly - strangers in a strange land. And I have no desire to organize them into anything.

Friday, Dec. 10th

SNOW! We will have snow for Christmas! Fa la la la laa, La la la. We are going to Uncle Jon and Aunt Joan's! I LOVE going to see them. We never go enough. It's always great, but especially in the winter. There is ALWAYS snow in the winter. They have a wonderful log home in the Sierras. I can already see the snow mounded up around it and the great roaring fire inside with all our drippy wet snow things hanging in front of it.

I hope my ice-skates still fit. Or maybe Janie or Jason will have some outgrown ones and Jeffy can wear mine. I am sooo excited. Bet you couldn't tell, huh. I think I'll start packing tonight.

Packing! Oh, that reminds me. Grandma and Grandpa Blair are leaving this weekend. Bummer. Bummer, Gummer, Nummer, Wummer! They'd made Christmas plans with Uncle Tim's family way before

Mom got sick. They were willing to change them and stay here but Mom said, "Don't you dare. I'm getting along just fine and I don't want to hog you from the whole family. I'll give you a call if I need you after chemo starts." I doubt if she will, but maybe they'll come back anyway.

Mon. Dec. 13th

Well, to answer your question, Mr. Moore, Uncle Jon isn't really Mom's brother, or Dad's. That's why he's a Kessler, not a Dixon. He and Dad have been friends since they were boys.

Aunt Joan is Mom's cousin, third cousin. They were roommates in college. When Mom and Dad met, the four of them started doing everything together, even got married the same year. They've just always been Uncle Jon and Aunt Joan, and their kids really are our cousins, just not very close in ye ol' gene pool. Sometimes they call Jesse their 6th 'J'. All of their names start with J. It made me jealous when I was little. Instead of Amy, I wished I was named Jasmine or Judy or Jill or even Jack! HA!

Tues. Dec. 14th

After practicing the Winter Program today
we all stayed in the center room, stringing popcorn and cranberries while Mrs. Mitchell read,
A Christmas Carol. She read the first chapter
yesterday and will read another chapter each
day, finishing on Friday. Today we actually got
more popcorn strung than eaten. Yesterday,
when it was fresh, we ate more.

Wed. Dec. 15th

Mom's just been wearing a row of band aides
since Dr. Long took the stitches out a couple of
weeks ago. But last night after her shower she
hadn't put any back on and when she leaned over
to kiss me goodnight, her robe slipped enough for
me to see the top part of her scar. It comes up
much higher than her other scar did and it still
looks reddish and tender and my stomach suddenly
felt all hollow. I wish I hadn't seen it.

Th. Dec. 16th

Thank you for letting us off school work tomorrow. The tree and rooms are beautiful. It's good to be able to decorate the school tree. We aren't putting one up at home since we are leaving. It makes sense, but I miss waking up with a deep breath of fresh evergreen smells.

Kesslers will already have their tree up and decorated, which will look spectacular as we come in, but you just have to <u>help</u> decorate for it to feel like Christmas. We have colored twinkle lights up in our windows and a wreath on the door and gate. That helps, but one NEEDS a tree. I hope C.C. likes her earrings when she unwraps them tomorrow.

And YOU Mr. Moore, have a *VERY*

MERRY CHRISTMAS

and WONDERFUL

New Year!

Monday, January 3rd

Oh my, another day, another year, another holiday over too soon. But it was the best ever! Sometimes my cheeks ached from laughing so much.

Kessler's house was sooo festive when we got there. A huge beauteous wreath was on the front gate and another was on the front door. No one makes wreaths like Aunt Joan. She'd also made candles with holly leaves and berries showing through the wax. They were flickering in lovely arrangements here and there.

Everything was decorated, EXCEPT the gigantic, humongous, monumental tree in the living room. They had actually waited to decorate the tree until we got there! Their living room is two stories high and the tree went way up, nearly to the peak of its cathedral ceiling. The bedrooms have an open walkway, which overlooks the living room. As we decorated, we could reach one side of the tree from there, but Uncle Jon had to bring in a giant ladder to do the top of the other side. He and Dad threw the strands of lights back and forth, Jon from the ladder, Dad from the upstairs walkway.

Jesse and Jason helped by fetching them the strands when they missed and couldn't reach them.

While we were waiting for them to finish the lights, Janie and I snuck off and she showed me the gifts she hadn't wrapped yet. She'd tried to knit Uncle Jon a pair of socks but she's not as good as her mom yet and will try again next year. But for this year he gets cool black socks with flying piggies on them. He'll love them.

We heard Jeffy coming and stuffed everything under her bed and hustled him off to the living-room where we draped him with gold tinsel and hung Christmas bells from his outstretched arms. We sang, "Christmas tree, oh Christmas tree, how lovely are thy branches," until he laughed so hard he made the bells jingle. Bet you can guess what we sang then, which made him laugh even more.

Finally, Dad and Uncle Jon declared the lights "perfecto," and we de-tinseled Jeffy and tinseled the tree. Then on went the balls and bells and cute little critters and all the decorations Jason, Janie and Jeffy have made over the years. It took everything they had to get that giant tree to shimmering perfection.

At last it was done and we all sat back, admiring and sipping hot apple cider with cinnamon sticks. Mmm, Ahhh.

Then Uncle Jon leaned over and gave Aunt Joan a sweet kiss and said, "Thank you."

"For what?" Jeffy wondered.

"For agreeing to this tree," his Dad answered.

Joan chuckled and told us, "Jon has always wanted a tree this tall since we got this place. But I've always been a stick-in-the-mud about it."

"Not a stick-in-the-mud," he put his arm around her, "Just sensible. What changed your mind though?" he asked.

She answered, "Life's too short to always be sensible."

A little cloud seemed to appear on the horizon. But leave it to Uncle Jon to dispel it quickly. "Is that why you've dispensed with your sensible hair do?" And he picked a clump of sparkly icicles off her head.

"Oh," she laughed, pulling on one that was draped over his ear, "I was just trying to match you." Then we all cracked up as we noticed all the silver strands hanging off each of us. Tossing icicles onto the tree had become a rout, with silver handfuls flying everywhere with more on us than the tree.

Sometimes I think that something can't ever get better but then, on down the line, it does. That tree really was the best though, and I'm sure it will be my favorite all of my life. [Rout (rowt) *n*. A boisterous and disorderly assemblage; a disturbance of the peace. A large and festive social gathering.]

Tues. Jan. 4th

We finally got a little snow at our house last night. I do mean "a little." It seems so meager after all the snow while we were at Kesslers.

[meager (**mē**·gər) *adj*. Lacking in quality or quantity, inadequate]

While we were there we had snowball fights and made angels and snowmen. Jeffy made the cutest little snow-dog on his sled and pulled it around the yard.

Dad and Uncle Jon had the best though. They each rolled up a giant snowball, and I do mean GIANT, higher than their waists. It was getting too dark for them to finish but I think Uncle Jon had planned that. He'd obviously been planning it a long time, as you will see. The next morning, he and Dad got up very early and by the time we got up, they were ready.

There were the two best ever snowmen in the front yard. Both had black top hats and long scarves and orange carrot-like noses held on with elastic around the heads. What? you ask. Why elastic? Because the heads they were held onto were Dad's and Uncle Jon's!

They'd hollowed out the big snowballs and climbed in from the back wearing puffy, white ski jackets with big, black buttons sewn up the front. Their hands were pulled inside their sleeves and were holding spraggly little bare branches for snowman hands. Keeping elbows tucked tight to their sides, they stiffly waved their little branches when we came out.

Oh my gosh! We laughed so loud we didn't even need to call Mom and Aunt Joan. They both came running right out to see what we were carrying on about. I'd heard of people laughing 'til they cried, but I don't remember ever seeing it before.

When they finally calmed down, Uncle Jon said, "Ah, lovely lady, I believe a kiss from you could melt this ol' heart.

It was a bit of a stretch over the big snow belly, but they both got their kisses.

Jeffy pulled his snow dog over and wanted a picture of it with the snowmen. They were so cute.

But that wasn't the end of it. Mom had Uncle Jon stay and made Dad get out. She put the white puffy jacket on Aunt Joan, stuffed her front for a proper snow lady bosom and she got in the other giant snowball with an apron and flowered straw hat. They were sooo adorable. We took pictures. I'll show them to you sometime, Mr. Moore.

Wed. Jan. 5th

The fawns are so cute out on the playground. Big Mama is not interested in the snow but it is all new to her twins who paw at it and snort when the little bits of snow spray up on their noses. There isn't very much, not even enough to cover the grass, but it makes everything pretty. Oh, there go the babies, tearing around Big Mama, kicking up their hooves to make the flakes fly. Big Mama doesn't even look at them. She just keeps her head down, munching away.

Thurs. Jan. 6th

Organizing thoughts for our essay about something we are looking forward to this year. Well that's a nice change from the usual 'New Year's Resolution'. I bet I know what Jesse will write about. I was there.

We had gone into Kesslers' shed attached to their garage to get the sleds and toboggans. Uncle Jon called Jesse into the garage. The rest of us couldn't help but stick our heads in the door. He pulled the gray cover off his big, red motorcycle. A sunbeam spilled across it, bouncing in all directions as it hit the polished chrome. Uncle Jon pulled a bandana out of his pocket and lovingly wiped some minute particle off the fire-red fender.

"So, my 6th 'J'," he put his arm over Jesse's shoulders. "I have something for you to think about."

"What's that?" asked Jesse.

"Where would be the best place in your neighborhood to ride this?" Jesse tipped his head with a puzzled look, and Uncle Jon grinned with twinkles bouncing out of his eyes like the sun off the bike's chrome. "When we come for Labor Day this summer I'm bringing Rosey here, with me. Your folks agreed to let me give you a nice long ride. It'll be your graduation present from me."

Jesse's jaw dropped and his eyes were almost as big as his mouth. "Anywhere?"

"Anywhere. We'll make a day of it. So think about it and map us an exciting route."

Jeffy ran forward and grabbed his Dad's leg, "Me too? Can we have a ride now?"

"You? No, you know Mom won't allow that." He tousled Jeffy's hair. "And Now? No way you little goose. You know I never bring Rosey out before the snow and ice are gone. It's too dangerous."

He flipped the cover back over the sleek motorcycle. "BUT let's get some transportation that IS good on snow and ice." We went back into the shed and he got down the sled and toboggans from the rafters. Oh we had SUCH an afternoon.

But I'm off the subject – what am *I* looking forward to? Well, the spelling bee of course, but I need something more original.

Fri. Jan 7th

Amy Dixon is such an idiot! I'm a *stupid Stupid STUPID nit!*

We were cleaning up after dinner when I grinned at Jesse and said, "I bet I can guess what you're doing your essay on, about what you're looking forward to."

"Well duh! Who couldn't," he answered, glancing at Mom. It was such a kick in the gut I almost had to sit down. She starts her chemotherapy next week. Yes, what I am most looking forward to is it being over and her being well.

Mon. Jan. 10th

I'm so drained, all leaked out and confused. I got all pumped up thinking about Christmas at Kesslers again, but it all went sad and cold the other night, and it reminded me of a shadow that lurked occasionally over Christmas break. I felt it at quiet moments when we'd laughed ourselves silly and paused to catch our breaths. Or sometimes I saw Mom sitting so quietly, taking it all in like from far away. And there were times I would catch others watching her with a kind of hunger, as if soaking up everything about her to store away for the future.

There were lots of pictures taken, like always when people are visiting and having fun, but a couple of times Uncle Jon made a make-shift stand with boxes or whatever was around. Then he set the camera's timer and ran and jumped in the pictures. He said he wanted some of ALL of us and I know he was thinking it might be the last chance.

I know it doesn't make sense. The doctor has assured us that the chemo should totally take care of everything, but sometimes that shadow sneaks up and grows and grows anyway, like a giant cloud.

The worst time was when we were saying good-bye. It somehow felt so final. Visits are never long enough, but we just always laugh and hug and talk about the next time. I can't remember the last time I actually cried at good-bye. I wasn't the only one either. We all just kept hugging everyone over and over and Joan had the hardest time letting go of Mom. Maybe she was trying to wait until her eyes weren't so red. Didn't work though. Finally, Uncle Jon apologized to Jesse that they wouldn't be able to make it to his graduation, "But that will give you the summer to plan your motorcycle ride."

Jesse really lit up and we all started talking about Labor Day and that helped a lot. Then he tickled me under the chin, "Come on Amy girl, remember, looking down will make you frown, pulling your chin up pulls your heart up, and yep – see," he grinned, "Makes your mouth turn up too. That is, if you want a turnip for a mouth!" Well, it's a 'turnip' now. He can always make me smile, even when he's not here.

Tues. Jan. 11th

Well, it's started.

I didn't know she was going in yesterday. It was easy to figure out when we got home though. It was like when she first came back from San Francisco, only without holding her chest and getting up slowly. She didn't get up at all, not even for dinner. Dad took a tray to her in bed. I felt so lost and helpless. There's got to be something – I stood eyeing the door of her room, and Jesse snapped, "Don't bother her."

I wasn't going to bother her! I just – just – oh forget it!

Wed. 12th

Dad's off work for a couple of days. He'll work this weekend instead, even Monday which is Martin Luther King Day. It's good to have him in the kitchen in the morning but not like having Mom smiling, "Good morning,'" at the stove. I think she was sick during the night. Maybe not. Maybe I just dreamed it.

Thursday, Jan. 13th

We swim tomorrow. yea. Gee, I can't even make it look convincing on paper.

Tues. Jan. 18th

Mom was up and about today. She probably took a nap as soon as we left, but at least it started everything out right.

Wed. Jan. 19th

Jesse fixed breakfast. Mom got up but Jesse was already mostly done and had her just sit down and eat with us.

On the bus this morning Heather plopped down next to me. "Wild horses, spy's with cute guys, or something funny?"

"What in the world are you talking about?" I asked.

"The movie this week-end. I can't decide."

Oh yeah, her birthday!

We really hadn't talked about it lately but I always go over and spend the night. The last couple of years we've gone to a movie in the mall and then out to eat, usually Mexican.

Thurs. Jan 20th

Endlessly - Unre**mitt**ingly - Per**sist**ently – **Assid**uously.

Heather was bugging me to choose a movie at lunch. I haven't paid much attention to the movies coming out recently so I suggested we just wait and look at the posters at the door and see what looks best.

I thought I'd better make sure Mom and Dad were remembering Heather's birthday and mentioned it at dinner last night. Mom said of course I could go. Jesse scowled at me though. What the heck? I asked him later what was wrong.

He said, "Don't you think there is anything around here you could help Mom with, instead taking off to a movie?"

Oh pu-leeze. I've BEEN helping in case he hasn't noticed. My room is even clean.

Friday, Jan 21

YEA! I've got a change of clothes in my backpack, along with Blue-Beary (we're sneaking him and Pink-Bear into the movie.) This morning Dad apologized that he or Mom hadn't had a chance to take me shopping for a present for Heather. Then he gave me some money and said maybe I could find something she would like in the mall after the movie. YES!

It's almost perfect.

Almost? Because Jesse has been skulking around, glowering at me from under his hood for days. I finally told him, "Look, I'll do some serious dusting and cobweb hunting on Sunday." That seemed to help.

Mon. Jan. 24

Assignment – write a short conversation without the word, 'said.'

I know. After the movie Saturday we went shopping. I've figured out the perfect graduation present I can give Jesse. Finding it is now the question.

~~~

"Gee Amy, since when are you interested in motorcycle models?" wondered my best friend, Heather.

"Not for me!" I laughed. "For Jesse's graduation present." Then I told her about Uncle Jon's present that will happen this summer.

Heather grinned ~~and said~~, "He is <u>so</u> going to love that."

"Yeah," I agreed. "So that model will help him anticipate what's coming AND in the future, remind him of that day and all the fun he had."

Heather laughed merrily, "That is <u>so</u> perfect. I'll help you keep an eye out for a red motorcycle. We'll find it."

~~~

We didn't that day, but I have four more months. I DID find a wonderful 'Friendship Bracelet' for Heather's birthday present. She really liked it.

Tues. Jan. 25th

YES! The list of spelling words is out for this year! They're not all that different from year to year, but it's always good to make note of the changes. Mostly it's good motivation; a friendly reminder that a lot of other people out there are getting this list and they are all serious about competing too.

The 8th graders were talking about their graduation trip at lunch. Last year's class spent a night in San Francisco, doing all sorts of fun things. 'B' had such a good time that C.C. wanted to do the same thing but everyone else wants to do something different.

Wed. Jan. 26th

Big Mama is trimming the old grass around the base of the fort. There is no trace of spots on the twins anymore. There isn't any snow left now, even in the very shady places. It might snow again tonight though. I hope so. I'd really like to scoop up a handful and feel it crunch as I pack it into a nice snowball - and take a bite out of it. Mmm. I can just feel the cold liquid trickle down my throat as I suck out the icy water, then crunch what's left between my back teeth.

Thurs. Jan. 27

[Disillusioned (**dis**·i·**LOO**·zhened) *v.*
Discouraged, disappointed, let down.]
No snow. Just cold yucky rain. It's supposed to be more of the same tomorrow. That means a long bus ride to town tomorrow with the windows all steamed over. Blah.

Mon.   Jan. 31st

[Preliminary (pri·**LIM**·ə·**nar**·ē) *adj.* Proceeding or introducing the main event.]
Preliminary thoughts on an essay -

A Changed Point of View.

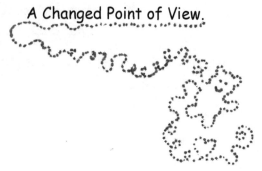

I don't know. So many things have changed, but nothing I feel like writing about right now.

Tuesday February 1st

I was opening my math book and noticed, 'Andrea Corbit.' That's something I can write about. No, not her, her brother Arthur.

I used to hate him. He could make me annoyed by just coming into view; always pursing his lips under his freckly nose, casting a patronizing look at the world, as if he knew SOOO much more than anybody else. Pul-eeze.

I couldn't believe my Mom liked Mrs. Corbit. It was her one short-coming, in my opinion. Eventually they stopped trying to make us play together when they visited, so Arthur must have complained about it too, the little twit.

He thought he was the best at everything, but by the time we got to 2nd grade, it was clear that I was just as good at reading AND spelling, as he was.

I loved reading anyway, but it gave me even greater satisfaction knowing Arthur wouldn't automatically have the longest reading list or best spelling test each week. Then our competition in spelling got stiffer and stiffer and he became even more insufferable.

That's when I started imitating him; tipping my head down just a bit and angling my eyes up patronizingly at my audience and announcing through stiffly pursed lips, "Oh no, Miss Abercrombie, I fear you have just trod upon a veluntia tar scoonum, often mistaken for a veltian tae snearum or common jumping spider. Unfortunately the veluntia tar scoonum is a rare and endangered species, and YOU have just annihilated one." How Heather laughed.

Then, in the 4th grade, both Arthur and I got to compete in a public spelling bee for the first time. It was WAAAY different than just doing it in class. Everyone thought it was great that we both won the regional contest and went on to county. Lots of people came to cheer us on. Only two people go on to the State Spelling Bee from each county, and to have both of those contestants come from our tiny little school really sent people bouncing off the walls. Except for me.

I mean, I was really thrilled, but I didn't want to share it with HIM. I wanted to beat him into oblivion. Until we got to State. It was awful. Santa Rosa is sooo big. The exhaust from all the cars gave me a headache and the hall for the competition was HUGE and stuffy from all the people packed in. I looked out there - row after row of strange faces, all hoping I would lose, so THEIR student would go on.

I couldn't see Mom in all those faces. I was so alone, squeezed in with all the other kids. I leaned forward a little and looked down the row to my left, then to my right – just as Arthur, several seats down, looked left. His hazel eyes looked huge in his pale face. But it was a face I knew. I took a deep breath, I could do this, I WOULD beat him.

Then as he got up for his turn at the microphone I had a wish I'd never had before - I wanted him to get it RIGHT! I did not want him to lose and walk off the stage at the end of that round, leaving me alone with all those strangers. I was more uptight during his word than I was during mine, closing my eyes, clutching the sides of my chair until the judge said, "Correct." Then I could breathe again.

Luckily, we both went down in the same round and luckily, it wasn't right at the beginning. The first poor girl to hear "Incorrect," was so distraught at being first, she headed straight out to her parents in the audience with her head down. That was when that horrid woman pounced.

Short and bulging with a weird hairdo from probably 40 years ago and bright red nails matching her garish lipstick; she bustled down the aisle, shoes clacking mercilessly on the hard floor until her claws nabbed their prey. She subjected the now sobbing girl to the trek back up to her seat on stage, with a lecture on the rule of not leaving the stage until the end of the round.

What a hag! Finally it was all over.

I was looking forward to ice cream and was NOT pleased that Mom invited the Corbits to come along. But it wasn't as bad as I expected and that was when Arthur and I dubbed that wretched woman Ms. Clickety-Clack.

Then we got back to school, and there we automatically stepped back into our usual roles and what I had felt up there on that stage evaporated.

Oops, writing time's over.

Wed. Feb. 2nd

So, back to Arthur.

Mom was very sad that summer when Corbits moved to San Jose. For her sake, I tried not to gloat and saved my singing and dancing for out behind the old chicken house.

School started again and he wasn't there and I was Sooo happy! Heather and Sheerese and Kitty and I celebrated endlessly. At the end of every month, when we had the school spelling bee, I was jubilant all over again. For awhile. But as the months ticked by, I realized I wasn't enjoying spelling as much as I used to. I didn't know why though.

Then I walked into the Regional Spelling Bee that March and looked over all the kids there, and at all the ones that came in after me. Something just didn't seem right. My mind was kind of drifting, waiting for the clock to tick down to starting time.

When Mr. In-Charge walked up to the mic I was startled out of my drifting with the thought, 'They can't start yet! Arthur isn't here!' Then I sat back stupidly, trying to push that thought away and concentrate on the words.

On the way home I thought about it though. I'd won, we'd had our ice-cream celebration, but it didn't feel right - like Thanksgiving without a turkey. I felt almost as low after the county spelling bee. I'd invited Heather, Sheerese and Kitty to come, and it had helped, having them out in the audience to smile at. But I had to admit, it wasn't the same without Arthur.

So that's the change I'll write about, changing from hating Arthur to missing him.

Thursday, Feb. 3rd

Kayleen and C.C. are trying to talk the boys into going to Ashland for their 8th grade trip but the boys want to do something more adventuresome than go to a play and out to a fancy dinner.

Everybody loves my hair today. I didn't have any homework last night so Mom and I had a "hair night." She's still not fixing her own hair but she can do mine. We did pigtails and poofy things and French twists. Then she said she'd always wanted to try cornrows. It took a long time but

WOW! As you can see, I left them in. I tried to do them in Mom's hair but the braids I made were all fat and crookedy. It's going to take a lot of practice but I am determined to work at it until I can make Mom's hair look as great as mine.

Heather wants hers done the next time she is over. HEY, that would be great for my Birthday. Say, hey, yea, OK. That's two months away so I can practice before then.

Friday. Feb. 4th

I wasn't trying to look. I don't think. Well, not at first.

I was passing Mom's bedroom door and stopped to say Hi, but she was standing in front of the full-length mirror glowering at herself. She was messing with the front of her shirt, fussing with it, looking at herself, frowning. She was staring at her neckline – her scar. Then I saw it for the first time.

It was awful. Not just the scar - the puffiness is all gone and now the area that was swollen before is all sunken in. My gosh, how much did they cut out? I backed away but could hear her slamming drawers.

She came out after awhile with a turtleneck sweater on, looking cross. I was pretending to read on the couch but I don't even know what book I was holding.

Monday, Feb. 7th

Monday - Monday
  Writing time

She's going in to Dr. Long's again today. Maybe it will be better this time.

Tues. Feb. 8
    No, it's not.

Wed. 9
    She was sick again last night. At least she wasn't up <u>all</u> night. I don't think. Dad took his days off in the middle of the week again. I didn't see Mom this morning but Dad looked terrible. Jesse didn't look like he'd slept well either.

Th 10
    Last night I went and sat on the bed with Mom and brushed her hair and braided it. Not in cornrows, just one nice fat braid down the back. She liked it, I know she did. I was NOT bothering her Jesse! When I got done though, it seemed like there was more hair to clean out of the brush than usual. Maybe not. I'm probably just being paranoid about it.

Fri Feb 11

I've been staring at this page for a half an hour now. Guess I'd better write <u>something</u>.

After I fixed Mom's hair last night, I wrapped what I cleaned out of the brush in a paper towel before I threw it away.

Monday Feb. 14th

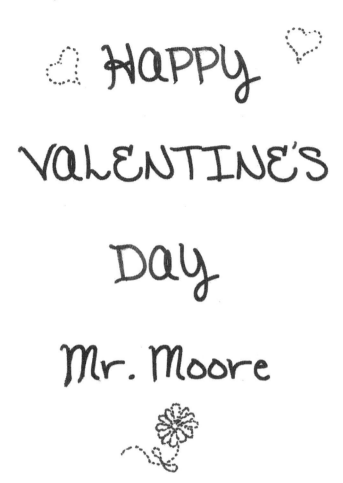

HAPPY

VALENTINE'S

DAY

Mr. Moore

Dad brought home Valentine cookies and yesterday we wrapped them in heart-shaped doilies and put them in with the cards for everyone.

Tues. 15th

~~Damn it~~ OK OK Crap. *Crap* CRAP **CRAP!**

Mom's going to cut her hair!

Her Long, beautiful hair!

She said it was no big deal, that most women have
a lot shorter hair. But SHE'S not MOST women!
She's MOM! I love how she stands out in a crowd.
I love the admiring looks she gets. It makes me
want to shout, "That's my Mom!" I don't want her
to look like everyone else. And now that I think of
it, she won't. It's worse – because everyone else
has hair! I know that's why she's getting it cut.
Because she thinks it is sure to keep falling out
and falling out until there's nothing left. She says,
"This way at least others can benefit from the
wigs that can be made from it." There she goes
again – why does she always have to think of
others. Why can't she just keep it for herself
as long as possible?

Weds. Feb. 16

I hate Jesse. He caught me crying out behind the chicken house yesterday and was horrid. He told me to knock off the blubbering, that he'd never seen anything so selfish and superficial and asked if I would rather have a corpse with long hair? How could he even say that! He is so Despicable! (de) - NO! I just don't feel like it!

Thurs. Feb. 17

[(de·**spik**·ə·bəl) adj. That which is to be despised; contemptible; mean; vile.]

Yes, that's definitely Jesse. He talks to me like he is hitting me. He doesn't try to comfort me at all. He doesn't even try to understand. Calling me superficial –

[(**su**·pər·**FISH**· əl) Shallow, slight, not real, affecting only the surface]. It's not just the surface, it may seem like it but it's just too much – too much – something – I don't know –

Fri. Feb. 18

I wasn't aiming at Jesse. REALLY I wasn't. I mean I couldn't aim that well if I tried. That's why they stick me out there in far left field, isn't it. They figure no baseballs will make it out to me, but one did. I was just trying to get it to the infield. Jesse wasn't even there when I threw it. He ran into it after I'd already thrown it. Probably did it just to make me look bad. And I did NOT appreciate Jonathan's crack about me getting up on the wrong side of the bench.

I'm glad we've got a three-day weekend. Thank you, Washington and Lincoln.

Tues. 22nd

I HATE it! I hate how everyone's jaw dropped when Mom came in today. Like they'd been hit with a stun gun. The only thing that was worse was how Kayleen gushed, "Oh Mrs. Dixon, I *love* your hair! It's sooo perky." Perky, smerky. She's probably just trying to drum up business for her mom, since she's the one that cut it. She is disgusting.

Wed. Feb. 23rd

Well, that's why they call it Dodge Ball, isn't it? You're supposed to dodge? I mean the whole object is to hit people - Right? So why'd Kayleen have to get all sniffy, just because she didn't dodge fast enough? And why's everybody looking at me funny? I didn't make the rules – I didn't break them either. So why'd I have to come in here the rest of the break?

Thurs. 24th

Mom's not coming in today, or swimming tomorrow. When I asked why at breakfast, Jesse actually kicked me under the table.

[Disparaging (dis·**par**·i·jing) To treat with disrespect, contempt, to belittle.]

The 8th graders are thinking about camping at Crater Lake. If they do, I hope Jesse falls in. Kayleen too.

Fri. Feb. 25th

I've been benched. Everyone else is in the pool, swimming. I'm supposed to re-evaluate my attitude. Well here's an attitude for you –

Go STUFF IT!

Mon. Feb. 28

AAAAAAAARRRR!!! MM

What an awful weekend. It's good to be back in school.

No – it isn't. Nothing is good.

Tues.

I thought this weekend would be nice - everyone home like usual so everything would **be** like usual, right? Wrong. Mom was so quiet and tired and every time I even thought of going to talk to her, Jesse just appeared out of nowhere in front of me, hands on hips, eyes shooting sparks. Not talking though; no-one seems to talk. Dad just chops wood and everyone is off on their own little island, even in the same room.

Wed. M. 1st

No one will play tetherball with me! I WANT TO PLAY TETHER BALL! It feels good to punch my fist hard into the ball. I LIKE the way the skin on my knuckles sting. It makes me want to hit it harder and harder. But no-one want to play and I can't play by myself. Even Gibb backed away from me when I asked him. And what did he mean, "Maybe you should get a side of beef"?

Th. 2nd

WHAT IS WRONG WITH EVERYONE! NO dodge ball, kick ball, soccer - When we were trying to choose a game at break, Kayleen looked kind of sideways at me and suggested chess. CHESS!

I took a walk and ended up in here. I see them all out there. NOW they play football. No one wants to play with me.

I went out to the tetherball and punched it, wrapping it first one way around the pole and then the other. Finally, instead of winding it the other way after it got tight up against the pole, I just punched it and punched it and punched it. Then Jesse was there. "Knock it off you little twit!" He distracted me just as I was taking another swing and I hit the pole. Hard. My eyes watered and I couldn't even move for a second. It hurt SOOO badly. He just said it served me right and walked away while I leaned against the pole clenching my teeth, trying to keep the tears from falling. I saw Heather start towards me out of the corner of my eye and I walked off quickly without looking at her.

My knuckles are red and swollen and it hurts to write.

Fri. M. 3

So I didn't feel like a spelling bee, so what. Besides, when I got "insufferable" and spelled it, J-E-S-S-E, it was supposed to be funny. I thought it was a riot. And, for your information, Jonathan, - Nothing has gotten into me – except food. HA. See, I'm a regular stand-up-comedian. So leave me alone*!*

Mon.   March 6th

I wake up and the first word in my head is 'chemo.'

I don't want to write

I don't want to think

I *don't* want to *feel*

Tues.

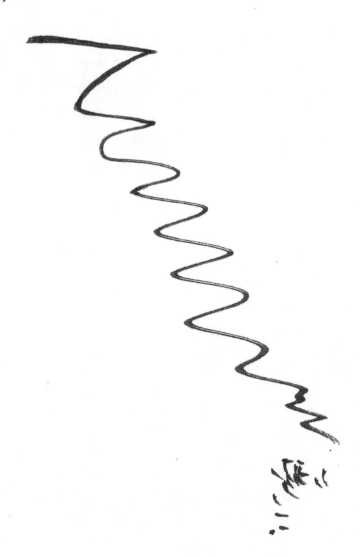

Wed. March 8

Thank you for not asking why. Not about the hat – I know you know the why about that. I'm sure that weasely little Kayleen has made sure everyone knows. I can just imagine her shaken, outrageous tones, relating her horrid mother's story. Why can't she just mind her own business. But the why about why I did it – thank you for not asking. I don't want to hear the question one more time – besides, I don't know.

Th march 9

I look in the mirror and I don't know who I'm looking at.

Friday 10

We are supposed to write a paper – confront ourselves. How can I confront myself when I don't even know who that is?

Monday, March 13

To thine own self be true.
But I don't know what's true.

Dig you say?   You're not making this easy Mr. Moore.

OK. The truth is looking in the mirror and feeling helpless, hating what you see. Everything you see: the puffy red eyes, the blotchy streaked face, the long brown hair when Mom's is so short - what little is left of it. The truth is hating what I see so much that I open the medicine cabinet door so I don't have to see myself. Inside the cabinet, along with everything else, was the scissors. I didn't think about it. I really didn't. And then there was a horrible scream and I looked up to see Jesse in the door, staring at me as if I were covered in blood. He backed up, gasping and pointing as Mom ran up.

Even I was startled when I looked down and saw the pile of hair on the floor like a little dead body. Mom's arms were around me. I was gasping for breath and dizzy. Then Daddy was rocking me and Mom was calling Kayleen's mom. She came even though it was late, and tried to tidy me up the best she could. She said to bring me to her shop in a couple of weeks and she'd work on it some more as it grew out.

The next morning it was a shock all over again. I didn't want to go to school but Mom said if a bad hair day was an acceptable excuse to stay home, half the working women in the country would call in every day.

I really didn't think I could face the stares and teasing. Then Jesse came in. I braced myself for his barrage of derogatory comments about deserving whatever anyone had to say after doing something so stupid. He didn't. He didn't even scowl at me. He just said, "NOBODY is going to tease you." He said it so firmly that I believed him. It was still an awful day, but whenever I felt like crawling in a hole I would look at Jesse, and he would look at me, and it was ok.

Tues. March 14th

There is such an empty hollowness in me - more than just my stomach. Like a giant vacuum has sucked everything out.

Wed. March 15

Wretched, that's not new, but it's a good word. De**jec**tion - Melan**ch**olia - Di**scon**solate

Heather is helping me with my spelling words and suggested I write the harder ones.

Why bother though. I'm just not a hat person. Mom looks great in a hat. She wraps one of the gorgeous scarves Aunt Joan wove for her around her poor bare head and puts on one of her hats and she looks great. But I look stupid in a hat. I can't go up there in front of everyone this Saturday in a hat and I can't go up there with this hair. I can't imagine not doing the spelling bee. I would never have thought <u>anything</u> could keep me from one.

I try to psych myself up. I try, I really try to picture myself walking up there being confident, but I see everyone staring and I can't make my feet move. The only thing that moves are the tears down my face.

What have I done?

Thurs. March 16th

I really love Jesse. When we got off the bus yesterday afternoon he stopped me. He had me set my backpack down then he pulled off his hoodie and put it on me. It's big and baggy, the sleeves hang over my hands, and the hood covers my head. I can pull it forward and disappear completely inside if I want to. He stepped back and smiled at me, "You think you can spell in that?" I threw my arms around him.

Congenial – **Amiability** – Harmonious - Mellifluous Heather got tired of the words I was choosing and wanted something more uplifting.

Friday, March 17th

It's really hard. I'm just not as geared up as usual. We have a spelling bee here, but it's not a real competition, like at most other schools. Boulder Point is so small; there's never really been any question about who gets to go. I've haven't had any stiff competition since Arthur left. That's the only thing that makes me nervous - not having anyone to measure myself against as I work.

Dad says not to worry about it, to just concentrate on the list. As long as I know my words, it doesn't matter how anyone else is doing. That's mostly true, but not the whole picture. It's kind of like a runner who seems to be able to find just a little more speed when someone is on his heels.

Last year Arthur was gone and it was sooo tough. I was struggling towards the end of the competition and if I had gotten 'supposititious' first, I would have gone down. But when that Teresa girl spelled it wrong, I was sure there was only one other choice. I have to admit it was a guess.

Knowing it was only the luck of the draw that got me to the state competition left me with nerves more raw than ever. And the first thing I heard when I walked in the door at State was Ms. Clickety-Clack, shoes as loud as ever as she bustled endlessly around the front of the platform.

Then I looked up, and there in the sea of faces on stage, were those warm hazel eyes under that crop of red hair. A grin burst across my face; we could DO this! I didn't even notice the "we" until much later.

Neither of us won. Some abysmal girl called
Sally June Something-or-Other. But we made it
to the final round.

I invited him to ice cream even without a nudge
from Mom. In fact it was even before we left the
stage, since we had to sit there until the end. I
slowly, quietly tore a piece of paper off. It still
made enough of a sound for Ms. Clickety Clack to
look around, searching for who made it. But I just
kept looking placidly ahead. She didn't spot me. I
wrote, 'Ice Cream?' without looking down, balled it
up and let it drop from my lap. Nudging it with my
foot I sent it rolling three seats to my right (which
were now empty.)

Even though Arthur seemed to be staring
straight ahead, he must have seen it out of the
corner of his eye because he stuck out his foot and
stopped it. Then oooh sooo slowly, he slouched
down in his seat, so Click-Clack wouldn't notice his
shrinking, until he could reach it. Watching him
unroll it out of the corner of my eye, I saw him
smile and roll his hand in his lap to a thumbs up.
It was the best celebration ever.

I always thought the old line, "It's not whether
you win or lose, but how you play the game," was a
crock. But I realized that day, I wasn't upset

about not winning. I had had a BLAST! Maybe it will be even better this year.

Arthur doesn't seem like the same person who annoyed me for so long. He told me that even though his new school was absolutely huge, no one was as tough to compete with as me. We left really looking forward to next year - and here it is.

Oh Gosh, I hope we both make it!

AGHHH - I wish my stomach wouldn't jump like that!

Mon. March 20th

Ya da da DAT du DA! It's such a relief to have the first contest over. The first one for me at least. I know most everyone else competed at their school before going to the regional competition.

Yes, we have spelling bees here, but Mrs. Mitchell has a separate pool of words she draws for me, and only uses the regular spelling words for everyone else. It's fair. It's not like anyone else even wants to compete now that Arthur is gone. So the others get to work on the words they need and I get to work on the words I need and it is more fun for everyone.

Last year Monte was in ecstasy when he made it to the end and I misspelled exuberant. Of course, his word was "blue." But I enjoyed congratulating him; he was sooo exuberant!

On another subject - <u>Finally</u>! The 8th graders have had a terrible time trying to decide what to do for their graduation trip. But Jesse came up with something everyone liked. YEA Jesse!

While we were at Kesslers, Jason told us about a way cool rafting trip he'd gone on last summer. It was in the Sierras, not too far from where they live.

Dad's going to help chaperone. He checked with Kesslers and Jason can go with them. Uncle Jon is going to see if he can switch days off and go with them. They are going to have such a blast! I wish I could go too!

Tues. March 21st

Everyone seems to take it for granted that I will win the county spelling bee, but that just makes it worse. Yeah, I love words, and knowing what they mean, and how to spell them, and yeah, our class spelling bees are a blast, but I never really think about them; I just get up and do them.

When I was little, if I misspelled a word, it just meant I could go sit with Heather and pass notes or doodle – no big deal. Then there was that time in third grade, the first time I got them all right and I felt like a blown up balloon with no place to go. I didn't want it to be over; I wanted another word and another.

I don't today.

Wed. March 22nd

I really need Arthur. He kept me focused on the words. In third grade Mrs. Olsen put Arthur and me with the fourth graders for spelling, then with the fifth graders.

I really liked being able to spell, but it had become more than just the words, it was Arthur. I had never cared for him; he was such a vile little know-it-all, not just with spelling either. If we were laying on the grass looking at dragons and teddy bears in the clouds, he would annoyingly identify them as **Stratocum**ulus, or someone would find a bug and he'd have to say something - like, Oh, that's an I'm-So-Smart beetle, commonly known as a Dumb-beetle and eats - well, whatever such beetles eat.

Once I muttered, "Oh, I know, it's really a carnivous-mundumas and eats insufferable red haired snots." He totally didn't get it. "No, I know it's a . . ." but no one heard, we were laughing too hard.

So the best part of the spelling bees was when I out-spelled him. Not just for me, others too. How they cheered that first time he missed a word and I spelled it AND the next one.

All that time we worked to out-do each other I felt anticipation and determination, but never once did every nerve ending in my body flutter like a trapped moth.

My stomach never took a roller coaster-dive. That didn't happen until we went to the first regional competition. I hadn't even thought about it being different and was totally unprepared. Oh, I was ready for the words, just not the audience, or all the kids I didn't know – the judges I didn't know.

There was only one face I knew up there - Arthur's - and then I felt something familiar; the desire to beat him. That's what got me through and let me focus on the words. It was the same at county that first year. I walked in and my heart stood still, my stomach was in my throat and I wondered how I could possibly spell out loud with my stomach there. Then I saw that freckled face under that mop of red hair, and every particle of me focused on, "He will NOT beat me."

I need him here to make me feel that again.

Thurs. March 23

I always thought that the more you did something, the easier it got, but that doesn't seem to be happening. Every year it gets worse. The more I win, the more people expect me to win. I don't know if I could face them if I go down. Yeesh, there goes my stomach again.

Fri. Mar. 24

Tomorrow, Tomorrow, TOMORROW*!*
My stomach flips whenever I hear the word.

Monday, March 27th

AAAAAhhh. . . **Yes***!* I DO love to spell*!*

I can relax now until State.

Tues. March 28th

Heather plopped down in the seat with me this morning with a way-too-smug smile. "What are you up to?" I asked.

"Maybe I'm thinking of something," she grinned.

"What?" I tried to tickle her but the bus came to the next stop and she jumped away and into the seat in front of me, giggling. She slid down out of sight, but a moment later I could hear her softly humming "Happy Birthday." I cracked up and at the next stop slid into the seat with her. We talked the rest of the way about what I might do for my birthday in a week and a half.

Wed. March 29

My birthday is the 8th. Mom has chemo the 4th.

I really tried to look like I didn't want a big party, but I don't know how convincing I was. I am sooo bummed, bummed, bummed.

Not really so much about the party, just wanting things to be normal and wondering if they ever will be again. I know there are lots of people who have to fight cancer for years and years. I feel like such a wimp being so tired of it after just a few months. And it's not even me who has to do it. I don't know how to stay strong for her when she's always been the one for <u>me</u> to lean on.

Thurs. March 30

Weltscmerz, that's German for dispirited. Reminds me of Dad right now. He has always been so caring and helpful. When Mom needed something done and couldn't do it, he'd be right there with his sleeves rolled up.

She's pretty independent and self-sufficient, so when he gets a chance to help her, he loves it. But he can't help her right now. Yeah, he's there, and can hold her hand, but he can't make it go away. He can't make it all better, like kissing our boo-boos away when we were little. He gets so distressed. I can see it. It makes me hurt.

Fri. March 31st

It's dark and gray and I'm beginning to hate the end of the month. It means the beginning of the next month. I overheard Dad giving Mom a pep talk last night. He wanted her to get some extra rest this weekend so she will have more energy for her treatment on Monday. His voice had a forced perkiness to it, going on about how rest and a good attitude going into it will make a huge difference. He's always had a thing about mind over matter.

Mon April 3rd

I learned something interesting today. The bottom of my lower lip is more sensitive than the top of it. I was staring into space, numb and somewhere else. I didn't feel the tear fall but gradually became aware of it slipping slowly down my cheek. It was an interesting sensation as the thick, warm drop slowly traveled the contours of my face, finally arriving where my upper lip sticks out, and then slipped around the curve. I thought it had ended up in my mouth. But after a moment it dripped onto my lower lip and continued its journey downwards. The whole time it had only felt wet and warm, but suddenly, as it rounded the bottom curve of my lip it tickled so much I had to wipe it away.

Tues. April 4th

I keep expecting it to get better. I really believe it will. So it's a surprise when it doesn't. Dad looks worse than Mom.

Wed. April 5th

He's HORRID!!! I hate him! How could he even think such things, much less say them? I mean, Dad has been upset with Mom before, but how could anyone yell at her right now? "You aren't trying hard enough!"? "You have got to pull yourself together and fight this!"?

You're the one that needs to pull it together Dad!

Thurs. April 6

Last night was awful. When we came home from school there was a huge pile of wood split. Not stacked, just all over the place. The maul was stuck in the stump but no sign of Dad.

When we went inside, Mom was starting dinner. She asked if we could find Dad, so Jesse and I wandered around feeling a bit lost. We finally went to the head of the path that goes down to the creek. We could see him down on the bank.

The creek is still roaring from recent rains. He couldn't hear us over the water, but we could hear him. It was awful. I've never heard an adult cry like that. In fact, I've never heard anyone cry like that - like every fiber of his insides was being ripped out.

Without a word, Jesse and I turned back to the house. Jesse told Mom where he was. When she went out, we didn't say anything, just worked on dinner. We also set the table as beautifully as possible. They still weren't back, so we went out with a flashlight to try and find something for a bouquet. The storm this weekend had pretty well wrecked the spring flowers so we went in and found some big candles for a nice centerpiece.

We were wondering what to do next when we finally heard them coming, laughing a little as they tried not to trip in the dark. They were holding hands as they came in. "Oh, doesn't that look wonderful," Mom sighed. Then Dad said, "Come here you two." We had a long family hug. Dinner by candle light turned out to be a good idea since none of us looked all that great and the food was a little scorched, but it was a wonderful dinner.

Fri. April 7th

Well, this is a great short notice surprise. Heather and her mom are picking me up tomorrow on their way to town. I'll get a Birthday breakfast with Mom and Dad (and Jesse) then Mommy 'A' is taking Heather and I shopping for a new Easter dress and then home with them for my Birthday dinner! YES!!! I really didn't think about getting a new dress this year. No way would Mom have the energy to take me shopping. I never even considered asking. This will be great.

Mon. Ap. 10th

I'm prophetic. 🙂 Ha ha. It WAS great. I tried not to be blue about Mom being sooo worn out for my birthday Saturday. I snuggled with her quietly while Dad fixed his special waffles for breakfast. Then we got up and I opened all my cards. Beautiful flowery cards (with money) from both sets of grandparents, a unicorn card from Dad's sister, a goofy mule one from Uncle Tim and an even goofier card from Uncle Jon with a grinning turnip on it; cracked me up. Aunt Joan also sent a beautiful scarf like one she wove Mom for Christmas, ". . . to keep my head warm on windy days." So she knows about my hair.

Mom and Dad gave me a beautiful handmade card with pressed flowers on the front and money inside for my dress today, "And enough for a tasty treat for everybody," Dad told me.

Then off to town with Mommy 'A' and Heather. Kitty and her mom ended up going too. We started at one end of the mall and went in every store. Well, every store that wasn't kitchen supplies or men's shoes. Snort.

After we were sure we had tried on absolutely everything of interest, we got some lunch and talked about all the clothes and which ones were the best.

When we were done eating, we went back to check them out again. I was torn between a bright sunshine yellow dress and one that was a rich blue with an abstract pattern angling across the bottom, resembling purple iris.

They said the blue dress suited my skin tone, even though the yellow one looked great on the hanger. Kitty's mom said it would always look great hanging in my closet but that I shouldn't wear it in this lifetime. Double snort!

Heather got a purple and lavender dress that was marvelous on her. Even better than on the hanger. Ha Ha.

One more stop for our "tasty treat." I got a bearclaw, Heather got an apple turnover. Our hands got sooo sticky. Then back up the mountain for an 'Aberration-Absolute-Birthday.' MMM mmm mmm! It was still sunny and warm, just right for a bar-b-que. Ribs! Sooo messy! Ribs have to be messy to be good.

Tory had a bone that he started poking his side with. Heather asked him what he was doing. 'Tickling my ribs with a rib." What a crack up!

That beautiful weather is GONE. Right now it's very cloudy and looking like rain again.

Tues. Ap. 11th

What a storm last night! All the apple blossoms that were left are blown all over the playground. It is still blowing out there. The trees on the hill are swaying like mad. Mr. Goodwin said he had to chase some deer out of the storage shed so he could close it up. They did <u>not</u> want to go outside.

Speaking of going out, the lights just flickered again. If the power goes out, that will be it for school the rest of the day. That would be great. We could go home and help Mom.

Oop – there go the lights.

Do we stay? Do we go –

We GO! Ms. Pascalla is going out to get the bus ready!

Thurs. Ap. 13th

Power's back on. The unexpected day off was fun though.

We set out candles for a little extra light, and because they were pretty, and played cards together. Then we took turns playing chess with Mom. One of us would play while the other cleaned and tidied.

Later we took the candles into her room and snuggled on each side of her in bed and told stories. Jesse was better than I would have guessed but Mom was the best. We had her tell about when she was little. Listening to her made it seemed we were right there playing with her, all kids together.

But here we are back at school and Heather says it's time to get back to my spelling words, I've had enough of a break.

Slave driver.

Ha Ha, just kidding!

Fri.

Oh my God oh my God   How can I even write this?

Mr. Moore said he wouldn't expect me to try
to do homework until after I get back from the
funeral but suggested I take my journal - that it
might help. But how can anything help? How can
you refill an empty sea or rebuild a mountain that
has crumbled? And how can I write when I can't
even see?

I've only been to one funeral before. Heather's
grandmother's. I remember being surprised at
how people could get up and talk calmly about her
and her life and what she'd meant to them. I'm
even more amazed now. I can't even complete a
sentence, like, "What should I wear?"

Driving, driving . . . How can I be so numb and hurt so much at the same time. The closer we get, the worse it gets. It's hard to breathe. I can't seem to take a deep enough breath to fill my lungs.

I see the mountains, looking the same. How can that be? How can anything on the earth be the same without Uncle Jon on it?

It was so very wrong. Just the three of them in a group hug. Right where the four of them stood at Christmas, saying good-bye - hugging as if it were to be the last time. It was. It's just that the first to leave the circle wasn't the one they expected.

Finally Dad broke away and left Mom and Joan still clinging to each other. They were quiet for a while. Then when I went back out to get my bag, I heard Aunt Joan say softly, "I've always wanted to be able to do everything, but I don't know how to do *this*. I don't know if I can."

Mom stepped back and took Joan's face between her hands. "You just do it. You wake up in the morning and you get up. Don't lay there thinking. Just put one foot in front of the other. You breathe in and you breathe out. You hold on to your children and they hold on to you. And you keep going."

It's late. I'm in Janie's bed. She and Jeffy are sleeping with their Mom. Or at least they are in her bed. Janie's probably talking Jeffy's ears off. She just goes on and on about nothing. Luckily she doesn't seem to need answers or comments to her endless verbalizing because I drifted off as she went on – the animals, stuffed toys, clothes, hair, people at school. She'll probably just keep going 'til she falls asleep in mid-sentence. Aunt Joan's still up, others too.

I can hear them downstairs. Is there really stuff to do? Or is it to put off that awful moment when you lay back in bed and your brain isn't busy with doing, and reality washes over you again like a crashing wave, smashing you into a cliff.

"There was a terrible accident – Uncle Jon didn't make it. . ." Make it where? It didn't make sense. "He's dead." Dead – what did that mean – a word to look up in the dictionary – to find a meaning that could relate to Uncle Jon. But there, there in the far corner of the brain - a hand waving - "I know - I know what it means." Vile little know-it-all, not to be called on. She can't be right. But there is no other meaning to the word. Another wave swirls and smashes. You try again to make it something that makes sense in your world - but it doesn't.

I can't sleep. I want sooo much to be asleep - to stay asleep - because waking up to it again is so awful. Maybe it would be better if Janie were up here with me. Her talking would help drown out my thoughts. But she might not want to be with me. She talks endlessly but she doesn't ever look me in the eye. Does she hate me? Wasn't I the one who was in danger of losing a parent? It wasn't supposed to be her. I know she didn't want to lose Mom, but would she trade if she could? Does she think, "God, you took the wrong one!"?

There's more people staying here now - his family, her family. Something going on all the time. And laughing. It doesn't always feel so mournful. Sometimes it's more like a party - food everywhere, people bustling around, talking about good times, sharing stories and laughs. Dad said that was the best way to honor Uncle Jon, because he loved more than anything to make people laugh.

I never thought I'd be able to smile again. Thought nothing could ease the knotted club that is flailing my heart and head and stomach. I still can't talk, but I can listen and smile as their laughter washes over me like cool water over a burn.

We were playing hide-and-seek. Luckily, Janie didn't want to. She's still chatting a mile a minute and would have given away our hiding place. So I was by myself when I ducked into the lean-to shed to hide. When I heard someone coming, I ducked through the next door into the garage. It was like falling off a cliff - stepping into that empty space. The gray dust cover lay haphazardly folded where he'd tossed it, thinking he would be back shortly. But other than that, the sunbeam lay flat across the empty cement floor. Jesse came flying through the door with a momentary look of triumph. It instantly disappeared. He almost doubled over as the emptiness of the scene kicked him in the gut. I slipped out quietly. Not to hide again, just to give him some time to cope.

Janie's in the bedroom with me tonight along with two of her cousins. She asked us if it would bother us if she read her homework out loud. We were fine with that. We've gotten used to her steady stream of chatter - well, blither best describes it. Aunt Joan seems a little concerned that she's not dealing with it yet. But if she can ward off the pain with words, then I say more power to her.

If I hear one more, "At least he was doing what he loved," I will scream. Or how about, "What a blessing it was so fast."? How can dying be a blessing? And fast? Too fast to say good-bye? How can that be good. For months now I have cherished every moment with my Mom. And even though I sometimes fail, I try not to take a single day for granted. It's hard having the thought of death hovering over you, but isn't it worse having it jump out at you unexpectedly? Totally unprepared? How can they not hate us? Hate that we were all looking toward Mom and it snuck up behind us and struck somewhere else?

The house is like a florist shop. Gorgeous bouquets and plants everywhere. Janie was giving us the scoop on who sent what, how long she had known them and every detail from jobs to toupees. She was in the middle of how she knew the huge cluster of daffodils with little forget-me-nots and no note were from Mrs. Whosit down the hill, when Aunt Joan called her.

I started to follow but Mom stopped me. "They're each picking out something they've given Uncle Jon for him to wear to be buried in."

Things seem to be going along fine then suddenly there it is again – smashing me into the rocks.

It was a little while later when I was headed upstairs that I heard them. I had to pass Aunt Joan's bedroom door. Jason was sitting on the bed holding Jeffy, patting his back. Aunt Joan was on her knees on the floor, face buried in Janie's hair, arms around her, as Janie rocked back and forth sobbing convulsively, clutching the flying pig socks she had given him for Christmas.

I fled, trying to out-race the rasping gasps for breath between the sobs, but the waves smashed up from the inside. I flung my bedroom door closed, trying to shut out Aunt Joan's words to Janie. How can she think crying like that is a good thing? How could that possibly help? Why couldn't Janie be allowed to just blither endlessly if that's how she wanted to deal with it? How could Aunt Joan be so heartless?

It was an odd morning - the house in a flurry, everyone bustling around, not a moment of calm. Every minute detail being perfected, more like it was a wedding.

Mom redid her make-up three times. My mouth totally fell open though when Jesse flipped out after some coffee got on his shirtsleeve. I told him no one would see it, he'd have his jacket on. But he started huffing and puffing and tried to wash it out. It only grew. So did his anxiety until Mom had him take off the shirt so she could wash it properly and dry it with a hair dryer before she re-ironed it.

Jason, who I don't think has ever even looked at himself in the mirror, was hogging the upstairs bathroom, endlessly trying to get his hair to stay like he wanted.

My hair? Well, that was easy for once. There was nothing for it but to wear a hat.

There seemed to be endless things for me to help Joan's mom with in the kitchen. I was standing on the counter, dusting the ornaments on the top of the cupboard when Mom finally said if I didn't get dressed she would dress me herself.

I was sooo glad I hadn't gotten the bright yellow Easter dress.

At last we were all ready and accounted for in cars for our long drive to town. No more futzing or fixing - nothing to distract us from where we were going and why. My tears were about to overflow when Mom started pointing out lovely wild flowers and oddly shaped trees along the way.

Finally we were there.
The church was overflowing with flowers and
people. It was a lovely service. The preacher
talked and so did other people, like Jon's brother
Dave, also Dad, and others I didn't know. Some
stories I'd heard and some I hadn't. We all
laughed some and cried some, and somehow it
helped, to be there in the middle of so many
people who have the same big hole that I do.

Afterwards there was a meal in the church
basement and more talking and sharing. Still lots
of, "What a blessing it was so fast . . ." and, "At
least he was doing what he loved..." It no longer
sounds so hollow and desperate to me.

I saw Janie talking with some friends. She
seemed OK. She was talking, but not blithering
anymore, and she was actually looking people in
the eye when she spoke to them, even me.

At last people started drifting away,
and it was all over.
                    But not quite.

It seemed like I still needed to do
something. Then Dad came up and suggested
Jesse and I ride back with Dave's family.
I suddenly knew where he and Mom were going
and what I still needed to do. Jesse came too.

Dad had written down directions and there
was no mistaking it when we got there. The 'T'
intersection: a little mountain road coming out
onto a slightly bigger mountain road, just past a
curve on the north side of the mountain. There
was a stop sign, but there had been ice that the
sun had not melted yet. The main road curved.
He couldn't see the big truck coming, only the
guard rail ahead as he hit the ice, sliding, probably
confident that rail would keep him from flying off
the mountain.

The truck driver couldn't see around the
curve either - then they were both there.

Dark thick skid marks from the truck as
the driver hit the brakes, trying desperately
to stop the loaded hay truck.

Red paint flecks ground into the asphalt
where it was drug.

Crunched glass powder twinkled in the sunlight.

He was dead even before the truck driver could jump out.

Fast. Yes, if you're going to die, fast is good. I'm glad he wasn't laying there in pain and agony in that twisted mangle under the big truck for the hour it took the ambulance to get there. I'm glad that up until the last second he had the joy of the wind whipping around him, flying along, loving his first ride of the year.

And so just the four of us stood there,
Holding hands on the spot where his life left his body, and we said good-bye to Uncle Jon.

Tonight was the last night at Kesslers. We were looking at pictures and having a good time. It started getting dark and I went to turn on the overhead light. I hit the wrong switch and turned on the ceiling fan instead. I went ahead and flipped the next switch over for the light - which reflected and shimmered and fell in twinkling strands, floating down to our up-turned faces.

Suddenly we were laughing. I was laughing - not just smiling, really laughing. Laughing like I had at Christmas during our tree decorating battle, which had landed that handful of silver icicles up there on the fan blades.

We decorated each other and ourselves with the silver sparkles as we described our Christmas tree decorating party to the people who hadn't been there. There's still an ache and an emptiness which will never be filled. But holding on to the good times helps, it really does, and Uncle Jon gave us an abundance of good times to hold on to.

The road unwinds before us.

Driving back is so different than the trip there.

We used up all of Spring Break plus some. The extra time helped.

I go over it and over it in my mind. Sometimes I could almost see him walk into a room or hear his laugh mingle with ours. I think about when we were saying goodbye and hugging, and it was actually less difficult than it had been at Christmas. Now we knew.

Janie gave me a long tight hug and said, "Thank you."

I asked, "For what?"

"For being such a good friend." Then she added, "And for sharing your parents so freely." She looked right at me when she said it, and I know, absolutely, that she meant it. She does not hate me, nor do I think hating us has ever even crossed her mind.

Monday, April 24th

School again. It seems so surreal at times –
too normal. Everyone is going on about their
Spring Break, little things, big things. Kayleen
went to a show in San Francisco, Shereese went to
her grandparents in San Bernardino, C.C. and D.D.
E.S. and all their family went to their cousin's in
Oregon, Gibb went fishing.

Most don't have a clue about mine. They just
figure we left early for a vacation and are so full
of their own good times they haven't asked. Good.

So back to organizing our thoughts for our
paper, "What Spring Sprang on Me." Well, I've got
plenty of ammo but I think I'll hold off to see if
our finished copies will be posted. I don't feel like
spilling my guts for everyone to peruse. I don't
need another dose of wordless stares from people
who don't know what to say, or even worse, endless
gushings of sympathy from the likes of Kayleen.

Tues. April 25th

Thank you, Mr. Moore, for accepting my journal as
is and letting me use class writing time to catch up
on other schoolwork I missed.

Friday, April 28th

That was good. Heather and Jonathon were walking laps with me, one on each side, looking ahead at the direction we were going. It was one of those silences that says someone wants to say something. A couple of times Jonathan took a deep breath like he was going to speak, but didn't. Finally Heather took the leap.

"We don't want you to think we are being cold and indifferent about what happened during Spring Break. Even though sometimes it helps to talk about things, I know that sometimes it's easier not to. We won't bug you and ask about it, but if you ever feel like it, we're always here and always happy to listen." Then we were quiet again except for the crunching of shoes on gravel. Then suddenly our arms were draped over each other's shoulders. It was warm and calm and peaceful as we finished our walk.

Mon. May 1st

I can't believe there's only a month of school left. I have no idea what to get Jesse for graduation now. Luckily, I never found a model of a red motorcycle because they might not have been willing to take it back.

Tues. May 2nd

Lost   empty - -

Wed. May 3rd

YEA! A bit of sun. No chemo this week! Mom knew, but forgot to tell me with everything going on. The person who administers it is on vacation and Dr. Long said it would be OK to wait until she gets back.

Thurs. May 4th

Jesse, Gibb, Alan, Kayleen and C.C. aren't here today. They're in town. It's Freshman orientation at the high school. They start with some sort of orientation meeting all together but then they each get to sit in on two classes of their choice. Jesse chose German and Biology. He and Gibb are hoping they'll get to dissect something. The school is providing everyone with hot dogs and stuff for lunch, then they get to go home early. Lucky dogs, frogs, hogs.

Friday May 5th

Well, they didn't get to cut up anything,
but they agreed that Biology had the coolest
room. Jesse and Gibb signed up for both Bio
and German.

Mon. May 8th

I had a bad moment in town this weekend. We
were in the grocery store and I was helping pick
out some fresh vegetables.

I was heading for a batch of parsnips but
when I saw the display next to them it was a punch
in the gut. They always used to make me smile. I
could hear Uncle Jon's voice, "Oops, there's a turn-
up." Suddenly I dissolved into tears, standing
there in the midst of strangers, sobbing over a
pile of roots.

Mom put her arms around me and resting her
head on mine murmured, "I know, I know."

Tues. May 9th

I was really tearing my hair out at lunch today. (An expression I can't really use with it so short) Anyway, it was about what to get for Jesse. I'd just popped the last bite of double chocolate fudge brownie in my mouth when Heather asked, "What happened to the motorcycle idea – couldn't you . . ." she trailed off as I choked on my brownie. Jonathan handed me his water bottle.

The three of us were alone on the grass under one of the apple trees. When I'd stopped coughing I took a deep breath, twiddled the grass between my feet, and told them everything.

When I finished and looked up, Jonathan had turned his head away, rubbing the back of his hand across his eyes.

Heather was bent over, crying openly into the front of her shirt, "Oh God Amy! I knew it was a funeral, but I didn't know who, and I didn't know, didn't know . . ." She gave up and buried her head again.

Jonathan took a shaky breath, "That's awful, Amy. I'm so sorry."

"Yeah," I agreed, "But..." my mouth stopped as my mind continued, '. . . but at least it was fast and he was doing what he loved.' I quickly looked down, covering my face in my hands because it would have been too hard to explain my smile. Instead I just said, "Yeah, it was."

Wed. May 10th

Dad and Jesse are coming to State YEA! They always come to the local competition but Dad could never get off work for the State competition and Jesse always chose to stay home and keep him company. I was dancing around celebrating about the four of us going when Jesse tried to burst my bubble. "You know Mom has chemo the day before you go, right?"

I'd forgotten but, "So?"

"Well, she usually needs some time to get back on her feet."

What a poop. I know she'll be ok, she never misses anything important. It'll be great. I can hardly keep my feet on the ground.

Thurs. May 11th

You shouldn't feel like you have to go to State
with us, Mr. Moore. Don't get me wrong - it's really
sweet of you to offer, and I know you said it's been
too many years since you had a student to support
there, and if you want to come, that's great. But
don't do it if you're just feeling bad about Mom not
coming. Jesse doesn't know what he's talking
about. She's coming, you'll see.

Fri. May 12th

What a huge dent. You wouldn't think five
people would make such a difference. The 8th
graders took off to the Sierras yesterday at the
end of school. They had accepted Aunt Joan's
offer to spend the night there and go on the
next day.

Today. They are out on the river right now.
What a blast. I can just hear them shouting and
laughing and feel the water spray over me. Mmmm.
Tonight, they will stay at a rad hotel with two hot
tubs. Tomorrow, they get to go to an old mining
town and pan for gold! Sigh. And here I sit. Pooh.

The substitute is running out of things for us to do, so he gave us a long writing time. I don't feel like writing though. I mostly stare out the window. Everything is so green and inviting out there. The grass is getting tall on the other side of the fence. That's where last year's set of twins are grazing with this year's. I don't see Big Mama. I hope she's OK.

Mon. May 15th

Since Jesse has come back from his trip, he keeps saying, "Come on Amy, don't get nervous."

"I'm not."

He said, "You are doing a great imitation, walking around mumbling to yourself, nearly running into things and dashing off to check the word list every little bit. You are making me crazy!"

"You can't blame me for THAT!" I laughed.

But really, it's not nerves, just a matter of being prepared. Really! I've given up trying to explain that to Jesse, or that Mom WILL come. He'll see.

Tues, May 16

I'm NOT nervous! I'm NOT !

Wed. May 17

I am getting SOOO nervous.

Thurs. May 18

NO! NO WAY! I know she'll be OK in the morning! At least OK enough to sit in the car. No one needs energy to just sit. So what if it's 6 hours? She's not driving. That'll give her 6 hours to rest while she's sitting there, right? Then she can rest at the hotel, then sit some more during the spelling bee. She knows how important this is to me. She's <u>always</u> there. NO WAY will she let me down!

Mon. May 22nd

Well, that sucked. And if you think I'm going to write about it, you are sadly mistaken.

Tuesday

Writing time. - SO - - - ?

Wed. May 24th

I'm still waiting for the lecture. I know it's inevitable. I saw the look on your face when you stepped out to grab me. It wasn't by chance that I slipped by; it wasn't that I didn't see you. I knew you were there, **so there**. That should lengthen your lecture when it comes.

Thurs. May 25th

Are you waiting for some lapse in my defiant, [(di·fī·ənt) *adj.* Showing opposition, resistance.] attitude before you call me in? Waiting for me to wear myself down? Wait on.

Fri. May 26th

It's been a week. It still sucks.

Fri. night

OK, I owe you an apology Mr. Moore. A big one. I'm ready to write about the Spelling Bee now.

I was really down about Mom not being able to be there, but she asked me to be a good sport and show Dad and Jesse a good time. So I smiled and acted perky and it actually helped pick up my spirits.

When we went in the hall, Ms. Clickety was clacking loudly as she bustled endlessly in the front. I heard you mutter to Dad, "Geeze, hasn't she retired yet?" It really made me smile, but not quite as much as seeing Arthur when I walked up on the stage. THAT made me grin - him too.

We were seated too far apart to talk but I knew we would get together afterwards. Suddenly I didn't have to pretend to be perky anymore. The clock ticked down and the hag clicked and clacked up to the mic to start the competition. I may have gotten nervous last week but all that studying paid off. I felt much more secure and confident than at the start of the last two years. My last chance to win here. 7th, 8th and 9th graders are in a different division and a different place entirely.

I leaned forward expectantly as the first person went up. I spelled each word in my head as the parade of spellers trouped along. Then came my turn. I hopped up to the podium for my word –

and got it.

For a moment I waited for the judge to lean forward and say, "Oh my mistake, your word is -- something else, anything else. Yes, he was leaning into the microphone – "Do you need a definition?"

NO! I did NOT need a definition!

My head twitched slightly side to side, mutely. I could not open my mouth, could not even breathe. I felt that sympathy tension arise from the audience that always comes when it's obvious someone is going down hard. The judge in front of me blurred and started to spin, or was that just from turning my head? The room blurred more, but not so much that I didn't know the way out, not so much that I couldn't see you step out towards me as I raced down the aisle. I heard Ms. Clickety-Clack hard behind, huffing and puffing herself up like a blowfish about to explode. I flew, out the door, around the corner, another corner and ducked into a doorway, expecting any moment for those red claws to slice into my shoulder.

Silence. More silence. No clacking, No claws.

At last I came out. My footsteps echoed strangely down the hall. Dad and Jesse were standing outside the door of the auditorium. Jesse's teeth were clenched but he didn't look mad at me. Dad gave me a hug and said, "I believe ice-cream is next?" I couldn't believe he actually said that. I looked up, still mute and gave another little shake of my head. "Well how about a nice meal and we'll see what they have for dessert."

We started driving north, went clear to the next town before stopping to eat. We didn't talk about it. Not then, not later. They understood. How could they not. I haven't talked to anybody about it. So I didn't hear anything about it either, until the mail today. I got a letter from Arthur. Since this journal is partly for me to look back at in the future, it's a good place to keep the letter. You can read it if you like.

Dear Amy,

It is hard to know what to say. That was not the day I was anticipating. No-one to roll my eyes with at Ms. Clickety-Clack's carrying-on, no notes, no ice-cream and catching up on Boulder Point. I knew about your Mom, of course, but it was still strange not to see her out there.

I hardly recognized Jesse, but was looking forward to talking with him too. I was looking forward to all of it, until you went up to the podium with your usual confident eager air.

It's amazing how everything can change in a split second. It was like someone had searched the entire spelling list to find the one word that would knock the wind out of you. I was absolutely stunned. I didn't realize until you took a breath, that I wasn't breathing either. Then you were leaving.

I found myself mentally cheering you on, like a character in a movie that you want to escape the charging villain, but it was real and you were right there and it was awful.

It was almost worth it though, to watch Ms. Click-Clack. She had a head of steam like a locomotive with a boiler about to blow. She was closing in too.

My heart was pounding! I wanted to jump up and shout at her, but then Mr. Moore took her on, leaping into the aisle, blocking her off, looking like he could breathe fire and shoot daggers from his eyes.

I wish I could have heard what he said as he leaned down to her because she deflated as fast as a popped balloon, and said, "Oh! Oh my. I see. Oh dear, oh dear." She kept on muttering to herself as she retreated to the front, her shoes somehow quieter, then gave a little wave with the back of her hand to the judges who were still staring. They called the next person and we proceeded.

My heart wasn't in it though, I just wanted it to be over and find you. I didn't want to win. It just meant I was detained even longer and a trophy was meaningless when my main competition wasn't there. I know next year will be different and all, but I hope you keep competing. Please, PLEASE, PLEASE*!!!*

Your Friend,

Arthur Corbit

So not only do I owe you an apology Mr. Moore, you deserve a huge THANK YOU. Thank you for sticking up for me instead of the rules. Thank you for understanding, and thank you for being a friend.

I know that you know that I know how to spell it, but just for you – Melanoma – there.

Monday May 29th

YES!!! I've got it - I've got it - I've **got** it! ☺ We were in the mall Saturday for Jesse to find parting presents for all the teachers and staff and graduation presents for Gibb and the other 8th graders. I saw him staring at a stack of something - starring yearningly, then he looked at the price, sighed forlornly, and walked away. When he was out of sight I scurried over. Electronic, tri-language interpreters. YES! That would really help him in German next year. They cost more than I had, but Mom slipped me some money and promised to keep Jesse occupied in the bookstore. He is sooo going to love it!

Tues. May 30th

YEA!!! A week from today will be Mom's last chemo-treatment! It's the last one scheduled anyway. Dr. Long will keep a close eye on her but he's very hopeful. We all are.

Wed. May 31st

Gee, my last entry. I guess things will be too hectic the rest of the week, getting everything ready for graduation and all. It's been quite a year. You're a good teacher Mr. Moore. No, I'm not just saying that. Have a good summer. See you next year.

OH! I just saw Big Mama under the oak in the field beyond the playground. She kept glancing back at something as she grazed. I couldn't see them at first, but then one scrambled to its feet followed by the other. Her newest twins! So delicate and tiny, but my goodness how wildly they leap already.

7th Grade

FRIDAY, SEPTEMBER 1st

Wow. What to say. Part of me is interested to see what it will be like to just be Amy Dixon, not "Jesse's little sister." But part of me isn't looking forward to it at all. I have to wait for the bus all alone now and it's the pits. As he was leaving this morning Jesse said, "Guess this'll make it more of a challenge for me to get the mail first, huh?" It was the first thing that made me smile in two days.

My summer? Well, it was a lot the same, except for the massive doses of sunscreen we went through. Short hair felt surprisingly good in the heat.

Kesslers aren't coming for Labor Day. They came last weekend. Dad says it's good not to get in a rut, no matter how comfortable it may be. So we didn't go to the river either. I hadn't said anything but I was dreading the thought of shooting the ripples without Uncle Jon there. Then Dad said, "How's about we go to the beach?" Everyone cheered and I jumped up and kissed him. He is sooo smart. It was a wonderful day. Janie and I buried Jeffy in the sand up to his neck. He was giggling and squirming and trying to break his way out.

At one point I was just sitting there, alone, gazing at the waves crashing and creeping up on the sand. Mom was strolling along the ocean's foamy edge. I just soaked in the moment - not desperately trying to retain it, just enjoying her being there, and the way the breeze fluttered her sundress around her legs and ruffled her short, perky hair, which is starting to grow back. Then I noticed, off to one side, a couple of guys gazing after her too. It certainly wasn't because of her long hair; maybe it never was. There's so much more to her than that.

She's done with her chemotherapy. Dr. Long says her lab work came back clear. She'll always need to follow up on it. Check-ups every three months for awhile. It's not something to worry about every day though.

As I learned this spring, worrying doesn't affect the future and there is really no way to know what the future will bring; you just have to enjoy the now that you have.

I was going through Jesse's language interpreter, (he said, "Oh no! Now she'll besiege us in multiple languages.") I found a great word; it rolls off the tongue in a very rad way. I'll write it in when I check the spelling, but it means - to hold yourself to the course. It's when you come across a stumbling block in life, something so hard you don't think you can overcome it, but you find the courage to persist and persevere; you keep going, no matter what. And I guess that's what we have to do in life, isn't it.

~~~

About the Author

Carlene Meredith Cogliati was born and raised in Kansas and is a country girl at heart. Carlene discovered the joy of reading very early and then the delight of creating and sharing stories. She wrote and illustrated her first 'book' at nine years old, binding it with pink yarn. A fourth generation teacher, Carlene has always been delighted by working with children, especially in helping them expand their world, their sense of self, and their ability to express themselves. She enjoys writing and painting and living with her husband and critters in the wooded coastal range of Northern California, close to a very small and wonderful country school, which is near and dear to her heart.